The Silent Summer of Kyle McGinley

THE
SILENT
SUMMER
of KYLE
McGINLEY

Jan Andrews

GREAT PLAINS
TEEN FICTION

Copyright © 2013 Jan Andrews

Great Plains Teen Fiction
(An imprint of Great Plains Publications)
233 Garfield Street S
Winnipeg, MB R3G 2M1
www.greatplains.mb.ca

THIRD PRINTING

Great Plains Publications gratefully acknowledges the financial support
provided for its publishing program by the Government of Canada through
the Canada Book Fund; the Canada Council for the Arts; the Province of
Manitoba through the Book Publishing Tax Credit and the Book Publisher
Marketing Assistance Program; and the Manitoba Arts Council.

Design & Typography by Relish New Brand Experience Inc.
Printed in Canada by Friesens

Library and Archives Canada Cataloguing in Publication

Andrews, Jan, 1942-

    The silent summer of Kyle McGinley / Jan Andrews.

Issued also in electronic formats.

ISBN 978-1-926531-68-7

    I. Title.

PS8551.N37S54 2013   JC813'.54   C2012-908062-4

ENVIRONMENTAL BENEFITS STATEMENT

Great Plains Publications saved the following
resources by printing the pages of this book on
chlorine free paper made with 100% post-consumer
waste.

TREES	WATER	ENERGY	SOLID WASTE	GREENHOUSE GASES
5	2,356	2	158	434
FULLY GROWN	GALLONS	MILLION BTUs	POUNDS	POUNDS

Environmental impact estimates were made using the Environmental Paper Network
Paper Calculator 3.2 For more information visit www.papercalculator.org

FSC
www.fsc.org
MIX
Paper from
responsible sources
FSC® C016245

To Emily, who gave me the courage I needed to go that final mile.

One

"THAT'S IT FOR THE MAIN HIGHWAY."

Well, whadda ya know! That's it for me too. From hereon in, there's silence. Complete and utter.

"We've still got a ways to go though."

My lips are sealed. My tongue is set on hold.

Wendy is signalling again.

I have had it. Had it, had it, had it!

"Scott and Jill are expecting us."

I, Kyle McGinley, have given up on small talk.

"They want you to call them Scott and Jill. They told me to tell you."

I, Kyle McGinley, have given up on talk of any kind.

"Scott and Jill have this consulting company."

Forget it, lady. You've had all you're getting. Nothing more is coming. Nothing, nothing, nothing. Zero, zero, ZILCH.

Wow. Feels kind of powerful. Like there's more of me. Like when I was in that arcade place, when I blew my whole frigging allowance—every bit of it. When I just kept pushing the buttons, seeing the score getting bigger and bigger. When I was laughing to myself because I was in control.

Control! Didn't think of that now, did I?

Just sort of decided, when I was packing my bag this morning. I wasn't going to do it any longer. I wasn't going to waste my time thanking people for things they hadn't actually done for me. Things they should have done anyway, without even thinking about it.

I wasn't going to make myself feel awful any more, saying goodbye, WITH GRATITUDE, to people who weren't even sorry to see me gone.

Didn't, either, did I? Got out the door without a word.

Control is something I could do with too. Control is something I haven't had, over anything, hardly, for quite some while.

"They work out of their home."

Maybe I should get real. Maybe I should admit it. Control isn't something I've had ever. Not so I can remember it. Not ever, in all my life.

"We have to make another right turn here."

Wonder if I can keep it up? Shouldn't be that hard. After all, Wendy isn't even noticing.

Let's check the watch. Yeah, yup! Been almost two hours.

Little shithead!

Should have thought of that though, shouldn't I? The voice that's always with me.

See you stick to something? That'll be the day. Kicking you out again, are they?

Only thing my frigging father left me.

Had to leave you something, didn't I?

I'd give anything to get rid of it. Anything.

Think I'm going to let you off the hook that easy, dimwit?

Just stop hearing it. Have it go away and not come back. Hell, what if not talking means I've made more room for dear old Daddy? Too bad. I've got to try it. I don't want to talk. I just don't want to. Especially to people who don't listen. Especially when I can't say what I think. It's like I'm lying. Lying, lying, lying. Lying all my life.

OK, so let's focus on the control bit. Let's think about not having all those words I'm always sending so uselessly into the universe.

Zapping them with some stun gun. Gotcha, gotcha, gotcha. ZZZZT, ZZZZT, ZZZZT.

Frig, how many TV shows have I seen with mad scientists in them?

Not exactly the mad scientist type though, am I? Although I do have the hair for it – wild, black, curly. I've worked hard for that hair too. Wouldn't you like to…? No, I wouldn't. I don't want it cut off. I don't want it tidier. It's the only bit of my appearance I'm actually attached to IF YOU DON'T MIND.

Always found the mad guys—the bad ones anyhow—scary. Often not sure about the good guys either.

Although there was that show on that weird channel—the show we couldn't miss. The one we all had to sit down to watch on Friday nights. Can't remember where I was quite. Just remember how the "mummy and daddy" I had there said the show was made in England. Which I could have guessed anyway from how everyone had English accents.

That show had a good guy in it I could relate to. What was his name?

Right, right. Got it! Doctor Who! Best thing about Doctor Who was his attitude. Style-y. Kiss-off. Like whatever shit he got into with the next batch of aliens he could always make it turn out fine.

Doctor Who made me laugh too. I could do with more laughing. I could do with a whole ton more of it in fact.

Come on, come on. I should quit with the fantasies. I should concentrate on how, any moment, we'll arrive. I have to prepare myself. I have to get ready, even if it is the same old, same old.

Perhaps on this occasion there will be something new for you.

Seems like someone is speaking.

Of course "someone" is speaking.

Isn't any "of course" about it, considering Wendy is the only other person in the car. And Wendy…Wendy is a woman. Female. I do know the difference.

Wendy is of no consequence. You have suggested you need a scientist—someone to assist you.

So?

I am one. At your service.

Holy moly! The voice has a shape. I can see him almost. Picture him? A man in a long white lab coat, leaning forward from the back seat. A man who's sort of bald. Sort of fussy. A man who's got a brightness in his eyes and a bowler hat he's holding in his hands.

Not the Dr. Who we had all those evenings. That's for certain.

There are others though, aren't there? Time Lords. A whole race of them.

A race to which I do not belong. The good doctor and I do have some things in common, however. I too find myself appearing often in places that are a surprise to me.

Like the Kyle McGinley head, for instance?

You could say as much. I aim also for an attitude that is somewhat similar to the Doctor's.

That, I wouldn't mind. Can I really go around with some strange being in my head though?

Mad scientists, Time Lords. They are all figments of someone's imagination. Probably you missed having an imaginary friend when you were little.

I missed a whole hell of a lot more than that.

Even your mother couldn't stand you.

My mother died. You can't blame me for that.

So, accept what I am offering. You have set yourself a task. You wish to not speak. I am available to help you. I also believe we might take more than a few steps towards getting that life-sucking ogre who is your father out of your brain.

"Life-sucking ogre," that's a good one.

There is, however, something I should make clear from the beginning. I am here on assignment. I will stay only as long as I am needed.

"My husband would love living out here."

What? Oh. There's Wendy, getting going again. Not that she's saying anything that matters. She's yammering on about how she'd find it lonely

"Although I do love this part of the Ottawa Valley."

Guess the Ottawa Valley's where we're going. Travelling, travelling. Trees, fields, fences whizzing past.

I'm confused. Big question is why—when my dad's voice drives me insane already—why I would even think of letting anyone else into my tiny brain?

Because I might be good for you. Because I am totally unlike your father. I am at your command. I will be gone in an instant, as soon as you desire it.

Do I "desire it?" Do I?

Shit, we're heading up some lane way, past some mailbox.

Remember the Doctor? Remember his approach to new territory?

If there's one thing I know about it's scoping the scene. I've been doing it since I was eight, for god's sake. Over and over. Regular intervals. Most likely I'm the world expert.

Lah di dah. Off we go.

Fact one: I see a house we're about to stop at. Fact two: the house has a downstairs and an upstairs where probably I'll sleep. Although it might be the basement. Been there, done that. Fact three: the house is kind of old and wooden. Fact four: it's painted blue. Facts five and onwards: beside the house there are two cars. The cars are small. They're imports. They're late-ish models. Fact whatever: one of the cars is red and the other's green.

*You **are** doing well.*

I told you. I have experience.

Pretty par for the course though. Nothing to get my boxers in a knot over, so far. Except there are two other buildings. Older and rougher. Hey, I'm in the country! The other buildings must be barns.

Good sleuthing.

We are slowing.

"Three cheers for us, we've made it."

We are stopping. The side door of the house is opening.

Out they come. Whoever the frig they are. Did Wendy tell me? Whoever the frig Wendy is. My precious social worker. Last in a long stream. Only known her a week.

Think, think, think. Scott. Scott and Jill. The…? The Jones-Wardmans! Wardman. Brilliant. After all, "a ward" is what I am. Ward of the court, or some other kind of garbage.

Is MY SCIENTIST gone?

I am not a creature of whims and fickleness. It is simply that you will have to work harder if you wish to keep me conjured.

I'll try to remember about that. Still right now I have to look the Jones-Wardmans over. Scott'll be the tall one, "the guy," most likely. Jill'll be the short one. Jill'll be "the gal." An "appropriate arrange-ment," one the Children's Aid should approve of. I guess they could be cross-dressers though. Or transgendered. Remember that kid last year in school.

Transgendered! That is something I would not have thought of.

Neither would I if I hadn't met him. He was kind of great. Whole lot braver than I am. Couldn't imagine….

Check out those boobs. Probably something I should keep my eyes off. PROBABLY should stick with how the two of them are dressed kind of casual, in shorts and T-shirts. Like they didn't feel the need to get fancy for this.

Not like good old Wendy, all social worker spiffed up, skirt and blouse.

You will note the male has his arm around the female's shoulders.

Could be important. Could be they like one another. Usually helps. There's a dog too. Down at their feet, looking eager, the way dogs do. Big thing about dogs is not to get too fond of them. I found that out the hard way. Dogs are tougher to leave than people. A whole lot tougher in fact.

This one looks kind of friendly, kind of shiny, kind of black. About the right size, sort of knee-height. Not too big and not too small.

Better not get stuck on the dog. Better keep the radar going.

Scott and Jill are separating. Scott's coming to my side of the car. Jill's going to Wendy's. A two pronged attack. I should get the door open. Get this bit over with.

"Hey, a Harley."

My T-shirt? Scott noticed? No doubt because he thinks bikes have to do with gangs and druggers. Why frigging else?

If I were you, I would try nodding anyway.

Couldn't hurt, could it?

Nodding is useful. It does give you time.

Might be polite too. I'm into politeness. Next step is to go to the trunk for my duffle bag. All right, all right. Can't help myself. I've got to give the dog a pat.

"Her name's Maeve."

What kind of a name is Maeve, for shit's sake?

"It's Irish. A warrior queen, not that this one's much of a warrior." Scott's giving me the details and I didn't even ask him. Score one for me.

Wendy and Jill are really going at it. Quite the gab fest. Guess I better listen, even if it is pathetic stuff.

Wendy: "I'm so glad we're here."

Jill: "It's not that difficult really."

Wendy: "The directions were perfect."

Jill: "It's actually quite simple."

Wendy: "Just kind of a long way."

Jill: "But getting here's always worth it."

Nicey, nice nice. Not much of a problem. Couldn't get a word in if I wanted to, could I?

Not-talking rocks. Not-talking's a cinch.

Here we go then. I've got my bag in my hand. I'm ready. I'm following everyone else in.

And I am accompanying you.

Is that good? Am I really sure about this?

I think you are going to have to see.

Maeve's coming too, of course. Dogs do that, don't they? Now I've started something. She wants more petting. She's pushing round my legs.

We are where? In the kitchen. Fridge, stove, counters, something of a clue. Not quite like any kitchen I've been in before though.

"We've got the coffee on." Scott's grabbing the coffeepot.

Homey, you might say?

Yes, actually, I might. Hell of a sight different from Mr. and Mrs. Household Products—where I just came from. Do I need to tell you that, oh SCIENTIST? Do you know already? Home! Home it wasn't.

The slight air of disarray would appear to be promising.

If "disarray" means books and papers all over, you're right. Big thing is there's a picture of the Himalayas. One of those panorama ones—whole great span of it—over the counter with the dishwasher.

"Sit yourself down."

Himalayas I can do with.

Scott's pointing to a chair. Jill's pulling it out, shooing Maeve away from under. Guess I might as well settle myself, take in the view. Wonder where the other kids are? Could it be there aren't any? Wouldn't that be something? Something I could do with. Couldn't I just?

No little trucks around. No girly pink things. Not that I can see from here anyway.

"I don't have much time, I'm afraid." Wonder of wonders! Social workers don't have time, ever.

Jill's bringing milk and sugar.

"Would you rather have a Coke, Kyle?" I'm nodding. Scott's heading for the fridge. "Maeve, basket!"

Maeve's departing, not very happily. Surprise, surprise.

Wendy has her briefcase out. So here we all are. All set for the takeover.

Coke tastes good though. Coke always does.

Scott's tipping his chair back. He's looking easy. Jill isn't. Like there's a spring under her. She has this pen she's clicking.

Not any longer. Scott's taken it away from her. He's giving her a wink.

Splendid, splendid! A good couple I truly think so.

Wonder how long you'll last here, little shithead? How many weeks this time?

How many? HOW MANY? Who are you to ask?

Mr. and Mrs. Household Products. Wasn't my fault. Wasn't me they wanted to be fostering. They didn't like boys. They even said so. They'd asked for someone younger. Didn't matter what I did, they were always looking at me like I needed hosing down.

Has to be someone somewhere that'll want me though, doesn't there? I'm not that bad. I specialize in being good, in fact. I'm the king of keep-my-act-together.

There are just these things that "happen." Over and over, like I'm doomed.

"We can't seem to find a good match for you." Which social worker said that? Was it when there was "the divorce?" Or when someone's granny suddenly needed to be moving in to what used to be my room? It's all such a blur now.

Scott and Jill do look kind of nice. Interesting even. Could they really be different?

I myself am always on the side of hopeful.

Good for you, dude. Do I even remember what hopeful is?

Moving right along. Wendy is shuffling her papers. "There are just a few things I need to go over with you."

Is Scott trying to catch my eye? Almost seems like it. Only maybe he isn't. Maybe he's just distracting himself.

"We did get lots of information at the orientation sessions." Jill's the impatient one. Not much doubt about that.

"I find it's best to be certain, especially since Kyle is your first placement."

The first. That's interesting.

Jill's smothering a sigh, at least I think so. She may be impatient but she's smart enough to try not to show it. She and Scott have this thing going between them. He's giving her a nod.

"What you should remember is that the Children's Aid Society—the CAS—is always here to support you."

Oh my god, how many times have I heard that? Say I was going to talk now—really talk. I'd tell them. That is the biggest pile of garbage I've ever heard.

"We actually have a twenty-four hour emergency service."

Oh whoop-dee-do. Maybe if you were really desperate, if you were going to jail or something. Otherwise, forget it.

"We'll try not to need it." Little joke from Scott.

"After all we're a bit far away." Jill's two-cents worth, at which Wendy isn't looking thrilled.

"Nonetheless it's something you should know about. I'll be checking in with you regularly anyway."

Not, not, NOT. I haven't had a social worker who checked in regularly, ever. I've been on my own from the beginning.

"About the money. Kyle's allowance will be part of what you receive on a monthly basis. If there are any extraordinary expenses, however... Let's just say we do have some discretionary funds."

"Scott and I, we don't need— We can manage."

Quite the deal, isn't it, people having to be paid to give you house room? You are a menace.

Wow! That's something. THE SCIENTIST is standing up to him. I'd have got a whack across the face for that.

Shit! I've missed a couple of steps. Everyone else is getting up, pushing their chairs back. I have to stay with the program.

Jill: "You're sure we can't show you around—just a little?"

Wendy: "You don't know how much I'd love that. I really do have to get back though."

Jill: "Maybe next time."

They're heading out the door. That's it then. Signed, sealed and settled. Package once more delivered. Kyle McGinley. Me. Kind of like getting a new stove really. One you can send back to the store when you want to.

We're all in the yard again.

"Good luck, Kyle. Good luck to all of you."

Wendy is in the car once more. Wendy is waving through the window. Wendy is heading down the driveway. Wendy is gone.

Two

ON WITH THE PROCESS!

Scott's stretching his arms up, like we have to do in gym class, getting himself ready.

Hell, he's tall. Thin too. His legs go on forever. His head's like a skull almost. His face… Actually his face is all right.

"We thought perhaps a barbecue. Get some burgers going."

Barbecue? They're supposed to be giving me the list of rules and regulations—where I should put the laundry, how I have to wipe my feet.

That does not seem to be what they are considering however.

Guess it doesn't.

It would appear, nonetheless, that they are expecting an answer.

Boy, can I come through on that one? Burgers were an endangered species in Mr. and Mrs. Household Products Land. How long's it been?

Would nodding with a bit more vigour do it? Should I add a little smile?

You might try something even more expressive.

"Right, it's decided." Scott's going in again.

Expressive isn't needed!

Jill's heading towards the porch. "I'll deal with the dragon."

The dragon?

I think she is referring to the barbecue. It does have flames, you know.

Why does each new place have to have its own lingo? Alien-speak.

Hell, she's got the cover off already. Hardly saw her do it. Need to face it. She really is a let's-get-on-with-it sort.

Still no sign of other kids.

Should I be helping?

Some help you'll be.

Your father is taking altogether more space than he ought to.

This space is mine, buster!

Listen, guys, I can take a lot but I can't take you arguing.

You are right. It is not useful. I will restrain myself since I cannot imagine the other party even attempting anything of the like.

I have to concentrate. Jill's turning towards me. "If I were you, I'd find yourself a chair."

Ah ha! Something I can manage. Have this feeling the two big wooden chairs have Scott and Jill's names on them. Seems most likely.

Not where you should put your precious ass then?

I'll go with beat-up plastic. Safer.

"We'll put you to work later."

I should give a nod in Jill's direction. More pats for Maeve. Good thing about dogs. You can always sort of hide in them. Be better if she'd get her nose out of my crotch though.

"For goodness sake, girl."

Maeve is skulking off. She's looking sorry. I'm sorry to see her going.

Oh, the boobs on Jill. Wish they wouldn't keep jiggling. Not where I should be looking AT ALL.

A cat's appearing. Grey and fattish. A distraction even if he is ignoring me.

"The cat's called Jim. That's it. You've met the household."

The other kids issue is settled? There really, really aren't any? Is my heart beating faster?

Jim is eyeing me, cleaning his paws.

A cat and a dog, that's all there is to it! This "temporary landing" could really be a good one. Hell of a sight better than most.

What now?

Something, I believe, you should be paying attention to.

Scott is standing in the doorway. He's wearing this apron. I've never seen anything like it. Front and centre there's a pink balloon face, flying about on little wings. The balloon face has a cupcake on its head. The balloon face is covering a good chunk of his chest almost. Its smile is so stupid.

You said you wanted more to laugh at.

Should I try a laugh then?

"Way to go, a man with a sense of humour." Did Scott really say that? Could it be laughing at "the man of the house" is OK?

I would suggest it is more than that. I would suggest it is welcomed.

Can't hardly believe it. Maybe it's a trick.

Maybe it is no such thing.

How am I supposed to know?

Caution. Caution and patience.

Scott's gone in again. Did he just come out to show me? Who knows about any of it?

Maybe I'll focus on the way Jill's turning those knobs, scraping the grill off. Except now here's Scott again. He's bringing a plate of raw patties. That is some pile. I'm practically drooling just looking at them.

"You're timing is immaculate, if I may say so." Jill's giving him a clap on the shoulder. She's planting a kiss on his cheek, even if she does have to reach up to do it.

"I'll return with the vegetables."

Jill's got a patty on the flipper. She's sliding it over the flames.

She's giving me a glance. Better get ready for whatever's coming.

"I am so incredibly glad Wendy's gone. Being on my best behaviour isn't one of my specialties."

Guess that explains the pen clicking. I was right. She wasn't a happy camper. Way too impatient. Something else to feed into the info bank.

Scott has returned. He's putting the vegetables on a little table. No broccoli, thank shit.

Jill is giving the burgers their first flip.

Scott: "You could get a job doing that, you know."

Is he teasing her?

Jill: "I've got a job."

Scott: "I mean a cook job."

"Don't get above yourself. You're falling down on your duties." Jill's looking at me again. "I bet the man could use another Coke."

"You are right."

Scott is going off. He's coming back. "Ta, da!"

The Coke has arrived. He's handing it over.

Maybe teasing is something else that happens here.

Oh, oh. He's brought a couple of bottles of beer. Beer can be trouble. Another of my life experiences.

When I drink I make a good job of it, you little shithead.

Go away.

Let them fight. I'm smelling that burger smell. The first bite can't come too quickly.

Seems like someone else is eager. Cats are such mooches. There's good old Jim, rubbing himself against Jill, gazing up at her.

"Nothing for you and you know it. Just you watch how well Maeve's behaving."

Hey, Maeve's sitting in the shade where the tree is. Maeve's all quiet.

"About that Harley."

What Harley? Why has Scott come to stand beside me? Shit, yes, the Harley on my T-shirt. Almost forgot. Here it comes. The lecture. About how motorbikes are to be avoided.

Probably should have chosen something else to wear today. But it's the best. Even if I did have to get it in that secondhand store place. Makes me know one day all this'll be over. One day I'll be able to do what I want. Including TRAVEL IN THE WAY I HAPPEN TO FEEL LIKE.

Today's the day I need it.

Still I'm braced. I'm ready. Scott's is opening his mouth again. "I had a Harley myself once. I bought it from Jill in fact."

"We loved it. It's how we met."

A Harley! They're not going to say any more? Jill's just going to go on dishing those burgers. If they had a Harley, they must have ridden it. Couldn't they tell me where? Couldn't they say what it felt like?

Words are on my tongue. I should get them back. ZZZZT, ZZZZT, ZZZZT. Remember. REMEMBER. You promised yourself. You committed.

I want to find out though.

I am sure you will be able to do that later. It does look as if you may indeed have struck lucky in this particular touchdown on the planet.

Could it be possible? Just for a month or so? Just for a rest?

Jill's pointing to the plate. "Why don't you come and dress yours up the way you want to."

Way I want to means the works. Lettuce, mayo, tomato, relish, ketchup, mustard, cheese, onions. Everything, everything!

I can see that Scott and Jill are drinking pretty slowly.

Probably wimps like you are.

That man is a broken record.

I was right about the big chairs. Good thinking that. The big chairs are where Scott and Jill are sitting now they've parked themselves.

The burger is fantastic. Juicy, juicy, juicy. A party in my mouth.

"Could we perhaps tempt you to a second?" Scott's getting up. He's taking hold of the flipper.

I'm into more nodding. A second for sure.

Hey, MR. SCIENTIST, are you hungry?

My wants are few. I tend to them.

Probably a good thing. Probably wouldn't make the right impression if I pulled up a second chair, asked for another plate. They'd think I should be locked away. Maybe I should be. Maybe I've finally lost it.

That's not how I feel though, is it?

I feel like coming up with THE SCIENTIST is right up there with the smartest things I've ever done.

Why shouldn't I have a figment anyway? What harm's it doing?

Where's the bowler? He's got a straw hat on his head now. Did I give him that?

Whether you did or whether you didn't, I must have something to keep the sun off.

He said he'd help me and he is.

He's making it so I'm not so frigging lonely.

Just frigging stupid.

I'm not stupid.

Well done, my boy. An accurate rebuttal.

That's it for the second burger. Shit now I have to pee. I don't even know where the bathroom is. What's that thing we did in drama? Miming.

Don't really want to act out unzipping my jeans, whizzing about in all directions, do I?

Control. Control.

Try standing up. They may guess what you are needing.

Scott's giving me the eye. "Second door on the right. Upstairs. You can take a look at your room while you're at it. It's the one beside the bathroom."

Thanks, OH SCIENTIST. Worked like a charm.

Except I don't even know where the stairs are. Perhaps if I just go through the kitchen…and the living room…

Yeah, yeah, the stairs are straight ahead. Good thing the bathroom door's open. Good thing "second door on the right" isn't hard to find.

Frigging hell. Seems like I'm going to go on pissing forever. I'm going to fill the bowl up, it's going to start overflowing. I'll be up to my knees any minute, there'll be drips through the ceiling.

There won't? All I have to do is shake the drops off? Why am I such an idiot? Why do I have to think of stuff like that?

I'd say it really is because you're halfway to lunatic.

I would say it is because you have an interesting mind.

How about I settle for that? So where is my bedroom?

There, where the door is open.

But there isn't hardly anything in it. Just a bed and a desk with a chair beside it. Like it might be for me to fill. It might really. Even the closet doesn't have other people's stuff.

Better not frig about too long or Scott and Jill will start wondering what I'm up to. Probably think I'm wrecking the place. Isn't that what foster kids do?

You should perhaps stop on the stairs.

Hey, this I've got to see. Those people, climbing up cliffs, standing on mountaintops. Are they…are they Scott and Jill?

The resemblance is, I would say, fairly striking.

I'm actually going to be staying with people who go mountaineering—with gear and everything. Another thing I need to find out more about. I'm putting it on the list.

Right now, I've got to get going. Through the living room again. On track. On track.

Hell, they have a lot of CDs. Good sound system too. But there's no TV? Is that possible? Couch looks comfy. I've always liked red.

Quick glance at the Himalayas. I really, really want to go there. Have Scott and Jill been? Could it be possible?

Kitchen door handle is kind of wobbly.

"The wanderer returns." Scott's raising his beer bottle. It's like he's toasting me. Better smile at him. Them. Jill's doing the same.

Seems like they're settled, like they're not thinking of going any-where. Do I really have to join them? Get back in the chair again? It's all right when there's something to do. Like eating. Now there's nothing.

"You can look around if you want to. You don't have to wait for us to show you."

Jill actually said that?

I can look around. By myself. They aren't going to start asking me questions. GETTING TO KNOW ME.

Questions are such hell.

Looking around is always, for me, an enjoyable pastime.

So let's go for it. Let's just try kind of casually heading off.

No one is calling us back.

They aren't, are they?

Can't imagine why.

Perhaps because they believe you are trustworthy.

Be something of a first. Not sure where to go. Not really.

I would suggest we begin with that barn there. The one a mere few paces away inside the yard.

Why not? They still aren't telling me I shouldn't. My latest Mummy and Daddy, Scott and Jill.

So here we are. The bottom's all open. There's a whole lot of junk here. Old tools, old furniture. I've never seen so much dust.

Doesn't look like any of this stuff's used ever. Except for the tractor. Tractor's got mud on the wheels. Mud seems new.

Who drives it? Scott? Jill? Mud might be new. Tractor isn't. I'd say it's as old as the hills. Doesn't really compare with a Harley.

There are also stairs and stairs must lead somewhere.

What sort of somewhere?

There is only one way to find out.

Actually, they're not stairs. They're more like a ladder.

Does that make a difference?

Seems better. Here I go then, up, up, up. The top's blocked off but it's only a flap thing. I only have to push on it.

And what do you see?

A great empty space.

A loft I believe is what this is called.

A great empty space with nothing in it, except that hay in the corner.

What am I doing? Why am I waiting? Why aren't I getting up the last two steps?

There's more dust here. My feet are making footmarks. The dust's different though. It has a different smell to it. Maybe because the sun's coming in through the window. Maybe that's it.

Gotta love those walls. Wood. Everything's wood here.

I'm out of Scott and Jill's sight but they're still not calling.

How long has it been since anyone came here? Why do I feel like...like it's been waiting for me?

Come on, Kyle boy, get real on that one. Get really real.

Why should you?

I don't know.

Why shouldn't you be pleased? Why shouldn't you be excited? Is there some law?

I guess there isn't.

Not that I have heard of.

As long as I don't get carried away. As long as I don't start believing it's going to last.

Believing that would be bad?

It would be a disaster. But I don't ever do that now, do I?

So?

Maybe not-talking's bringing me luck.

It is what you have chosen. Control, remember?

The loft's so big. I could do a couple of cartwheels.

Then why don't you?

Only thing in gym class I can do. My specialty.

As you noticed, you have more than enough space.

I could go round and round. I could, sort of, be like I'm in a circus.

You could but you are still standing there.

No, I'm not. First one wasn't so good but now I've got the rhythm. I've got that kind of spring thing that's the key.

Over, over, over.

Great, great, great.

And…back on my feet.

Here go my arms up, like it's the Olympics, like I'm accepting a cheer.

The gold medal is mine.

You want to know what's best? Best is Scott and Jill still aren't yelling for me. They still don't want to reel me in.

Maybe I'll go back though. I don't want them getting suspicious. About anything. I do like this ladder.

Somehow the dishes and stuff have got cleared away in my absence.

Looks like Scott and Jill were thinking of moving anyway. They're both of them on their feet. Scott's stretching again. "We were wondering about a walk."

Maeve's sure up for it. Look at that tail going.

Jill: "After all we need to introduce you to the scenery."

I guess a walk is something I can handle. But I've hardly seen the house yet.

It would seem for Scott and Jill the outdoors is important.

We're going towards a gate. Scott is opening it. "Rule number one."

So there are rules.

Jill: "This gate gets opened. This gate gets closed."

Scott: "Leave it open and we have cattle up the ying yang."

A rule but a rule that seems sensible.

Cattle? There are cattle?

This is a farm.

Cattle! Am I going to have to be a cowboy? Am I going to have to ride a horse? Can I? Would I like to?

Can't get over it. Whole new world.

Three

SHIT, I'VE SLEPT IN.

No, no. I haven't. As I can see from the trusty little alarm clock I always bring with me. The alarm clock I set up on the night table before I went to bed. It isn't even that late.

So where the hell am I? Walls are bare. No smiling Jesus.

Got it, got it, got it. Mr. and Mrs. Household Products are behind me.

I am AT THE JONES-WARDMANS. I AM AT SCOTT AND JILL'S.

And they...they told me I could get up when I wanted to.

Lazy little asshole.

They'd said they'd be working. They told me...they told me they're into ecology. They have some big project on.

Scott'll be out. He'll be...be inspecting some site.

Right, right. I heard them, didn't I, when they got up? Not that they weren't quiet. They were because here there aren't any other kids to be waking, feeding, organizing. It's just them, the two of them, all by themselves.

All I had to do was turn over, close my eyes again. I've had a good night. Don't usually in new places. Too many creaks I don't recognize.

Meaning you must have had more than your fair share of insomnia.

Hey, THE SCIENTIST! He's twirling his little bowler. Shouldn't forget about him, now should I? One more new slice of life.

Still has his lab coat on. Looks like he's been awake awhile.

I am ever vigilant.

Straw hat's gone. Weird how I'm so pleased to see him.

You did after all conjure me.

Mustn't forget that either.

THE SCIENTIST is here because I have given up on speaking. ZZZZT, ZZZZT, ZZZZT, ZZZZT. ZAP, ZAP, ZAP.

If I am to stay I should be given a name.

But I've only just woken up. My brain's not in gear yet.

Do not forget I am your figment. I shall answer to the name of your choosing.

Fine. I'd rather choose something you like though.

That is most generous.

Too pathetic to think of anything for yourself, more likely.

Let us both ignore that.

So, what should it be?

I am going to admit something to you.

OK by me, man.

The truth is I have always wanted to be known as the Lord of Ingenuity.

If that's what you want, bro.

It is, however, rather a mouthful. Somewhat cumbersome.

Could we try Ingen for short?

The perfect solution. I am delighted.

Finally, I've managed to please someone.

Shall we arise, perhaps, start the day?

Probably better.

My son, the loony.

We'll ignore that also.

We will get our legs out from under the duvet. We will? I will. There is only one of me.

Hot in the night. Hot yesterday, now I come to think about it. Which I didn't then. I was too busy.

Better give up on the Harley shirt, seeing as how I went to bed in it. Probably stinks.

Should I unpack? No, I'll just grab something out of the duffle bag. Perfect. Howard Street School. Crest and everything. When the hell was I there? Or did I somehow "inherit it?" From some other Howard Street School kid where I was living?

Harley is tempting. Maybe if I wore it I'd learn more about how Scott and Jill used to have one. Where they went on it. I'll check the armpits. Wow! Howard Street it is.

Quick trip to the bathroom. Now I know where the bathroom is and all.

Ingen do you have to…?

That is no concern of yours.

It might be.

You have no need to worry. I tend to my own wants. I told you.

Get a load of those mountains, still on the stairs there. Have a better look at those crags. More importantly, brace myself for human contact.

All right so far. The living room is still there where I thought it should be. House doesn't seem to have changed overnight. Still can't see why they've got that picture of teacups on the wall though. Looks like someone painted it. Could it be what you'd call "art?"

Can't hear anything from the office. Can't see anyone in there either.

Know where the office is now, don't I? Did get to go on the house tour in the end. I know how to load the dishwasher. I know I can read any book I want to. I can play the CDs as long as I keep the sound down during work times. I also know there really, really, REALLY isn't any TV, although there is a monitor in some cupboard for watching movies now and then.

Got all that after we'd come back from the fields.

Where you learned you did not have to be a cowboy.

Exactly, exactly.

Amazing how it all happened. I still didn't have to say a word. It just got easier and easier. Just listening. Why did I bother talking ever? When NOT is so much more restful.

Of course, there was that nasty moment when Jill asked me if I thought they talked too much. Kind of knew what she was getting at, didn't I?

Still, all I had to do was shake my head and shrug. Scott was right in there: "We need to be sure you know you are allowed to get a word or two in edgewise. We're all too good at filling the spaces."

Felt like he was bailing me out almost. Could it be he was?

Don't expect so. Doesn't seem too likely.

Hell, I'm hungry.

The kitchen is probably the best bet in that case!

Go figure!

The kitchen is where I'm going. Oh, oh. Jill's there already. She's standing by the sink. I was hoping I wouldn't have to see anyone.

Too late to sneak back. She's got me on her radar.

"Sleep OK?"

I'm giving her the once over, checking to see if she's turned into a werewolf overnight. Hasn't happened anywhere I've been so far. Never know though.

Moron.

Not much change. Same clothes almost. Same short hair, same freckles. Same boobs I shouldn't look at.

No fangs, no hairy cheeks, no pointy teeth.

Kitchen's the same too, chairs, round table, centre island. Himalayas!

Oh, oh, should've noticed. Jill's worried. Maybe I should've got up earlier. Maybe they didn't mean it when they said I could sleep in.

"I was wondering if perhaps I should come and wake you."

Let's try an apologetic face. Might be helpful.

"In the end I figured I should get my act together first. I was so angry."

But they told me I didn't have to get up till I wanted.

Wouldn't be the first time though, would it? Yesterday heaven, today…today…

Not that the heavens have been that frequent.

"I was making myself a coffee. Giving myself a talking to."

Here I go. I'm looking even sorrier.

"Kyle, Kyle, it's not you I'm angry with."

Who else is there?

"There's been a message from Wendy."

Wendy? Wendy? But why? When I left good old Mr. and Mrs. Household Products, I was careful. The room was tidy. I hadn't broken anything. I didn't leave my dirty socks behind me.

Listen, listen.

All right for you, oh Ingen. My head's spinning.

Breathe, breathe.

Jill's got her fist clenched. She's sort of driving it into the counter. "I wanted her to talk to you herself but she said she had some meeting she had to be at."

Figures.

"I wanted her to wait but she seemed to think we needed to know about this at once. Why, I'm not sure."

Could say that makes two of us.

"I don't understand any of it."

I don't even know what any of it's about.

Here's good old Jim-cat. He's jumping up on the table. Where's Maeve? Outside? Jim's a good substitute. His fur's so soft.

Jill's turning away. No, she's turning back again.

I'm waiting. WAITING.

"Wendy wanted us to know there's been a message from your father."

That has to be bullshit.

Remember me, your dear old daddy!

Why would Jill be saying it though?

"I gather he hasn't contacted you since he left."

She's right on that. I haven't had so much as a frigging postcard from him. Not since the day when I was sitting on that doorstep for god's sake. Eight frigging years old.

Maybe Ingen was the first sign. Maybe I really am going nutso. I've got to be imagining what Jill's telling me. I've got to be making it up.

It's weird too. Jill's so angry. "And now it's just a letter from his lawyer. I don't understand how he could do that." She's shaking her head. Her voice is trembling.

But she's angry for me.

Could it be what she's telling me is for real?

"The thing is the letter doesn't even say anything. It's a sort of a notification of your father's presence. Wendy says she'll send it. I truly, truly don't see how he could do that. Not after all this time."

Maybe that's something I do get. My dad's the king of mind games.

Feels like I'm going to have to believe this.

Jill's shaking her head at me. "It must be a shock."

Shock? Shock? I am nodding, admitting it. I'm not telling her my guts have turned to water. I'm not letting her know I've got a horrible salt taste in my mouth.

I've got to get out of here. I've got to do it quickly.

Careful. Careful

What are you saying? No, no, you're right. I don't want Jill knowing I'm upset. I don't want anyone knowing that ever.

Swallow, swallow. I'm going to have to go through the motions. Nod, smile, shrug.

"I'm sorry about this. I am really. Can I make you some toast or something?"

Toast. Can I manage it? Going to have to try.

She's putting the bread in. And I am eating.

Duh!!

I'm proving to her I'm cool. I can handle this. I'm drinking some OJ as well.

"Did you want to call Wendy maybe?"

No, no I don't. I want—

How can I tell her?

You could point through the window.

I could. I am.

I'm somehow sort of showing her what I want to do is…is be by myself a while. Maybe go through the gate we went through yesterday. Have another a walk.

"You're sure you don't want to talk about it?"

I'm shaking my head.

I would suggest not too violently.

I'm focussing on gently.

"I could come with you."

I don't need that.

"I don't like this. Not when you've only just got here."

How to show her I won't be long? I won't. I won't really.

"But there must be something I can do for you."

Why doesn't she stop this? Why doesn't she just leave me alone?

Her behaviour is, in fact, quite normal.

Maybe it is but…

"It's hard when you don't even really know us. When we're such strangers."

Strangers! That's it. The reason.

Also you're a freak.

Strangers. Frantic nodding.

"Would you like to take Maeve?"

No, no, I wouldn't.

I don't want to be responsible for anything. Can't say that though, can I?

"All right, I'll stop nagging."

Smiling's getting more difficult but I can do it. I can even look grateful. I can deal with the wonky door handle.

I'm gone. I've made my escape. I'm in the yard.

I'm walking—slowly, in case Jill's watching me from the window. Where am I going? Am I going to the barn, the loft?

No, it's too close. I've got to go further.

The gate. The gate. I have to get to that. I have to open it AND I HAVE TO CLOSE IT. I have to turn, give a wave.

Get myself past the second barn now. The one Scott said is where the cattle will go in the winter. Smell the cow shit smell of it.

Oh, oh, here it comes. My stomach's churning. I'm retching.

I'm diving behind a bush.

Heave. Heave. Breakfast is returning. I'm chucking my guts up. My guts, my guts.

Four

TASTE IN MY MOUTH IS AWFUL. UPCHUCK STINKS.

I'm sweating, shaking. I need water.

Steady, my boy, steady.

My teeth are chattering.

I can see it all again too, can't I?

Thought I'd stopped that. All the memories. Thought I wasn't going to have go over it. Not ever. EVER, EVER, EVER AGAIN. Worked hard for that.

Here I am though. Little kid. Waiting.

Stupid little sucker.

Here it comes too. The movie of it, filling up my head.

I may be behind the bush but I can hear the words still. Mrs. Smith with the red hair that babysat me.

> She's got the phone in her hands. She's talking to someone at dear old daddy's office. "What do you mean he's gone out of town? He told me I'd be keeping his son for the afternoon."
>
> She won't let me in. She doesn't want me. It's getting later, colder.
>
> I'm starting to look for him. I'm taking matters into my own hands. But I don't know the streets well. There's a police car. "We've been searching for you, son."
>
> That's it. The police are picking me up. They're taking me to the station. I don't know anyone there. NOT ANYONE.

Perhaps if you would just start walking again.

Walking?

Travelling the landscape, looking around you.

There was that other woman who came. A social worker. Who else would it be? I didn't know her either. She took me to some place—a group home or something—where there were other kids. I didn't know them. I didn't know where I was even. I could have been on Mars.

I wanted to go back to our home. I knew we had stuff there. I was sure my dad would come to get it. I was sure that's how I'd find him. And I had to find him because no one else could. No one else knew either where he'd gone.

I asked. No one would let me go. No one would let me do anything I wanted. They just kept telling me I was going to be cared for.

I didn't want to be cared for.

Steady, steady. You have started running.

Running's all right. I'm going to keep on doing it.

There are the cattle. They need to be considered.

Cattle don't look like they're bothered. Cattle are just standing there, munching. I don't have to be a cowboy, do I?

No, you do not.

Why doesn't it stop? The memory. I don't want it back again. All those things I said.

Dad, Dad, I'm sorry. Dad, Dad, Dad, I didn't mean to spill my cornflakes.

All the things he said to me.

Kiss you goodbye? Why would I?

I won't again. I won't ever.

I promise. I PROMISE. I PROMISE.

Fathers don't leave because you spill the milk at breakfast. Mine did. Who knows if he'd been planning it or if he hadn't.

Careful, careful. Watch where you put your feet.

How can I watch? How can I keep out of the cow shit even when…

Ingen, you don't get it. You weren't there.

My dad's voice, when it comes now, it's nothing. Then, when I was with him, it was all the time. You should've heard it. He was at me. At me and at me. And he's so strong. His hands can hurt you.

There wasn't only his voice though, was there? There was mine. I was always begging.

> Don't put me in the closet. Don't put me in the closet, please.

I could beg all I liked. Never made any difference.

Someone's got to teach you.

I'd be there hours. My father would go out. He'd leave me. I wouldn't know even then when he was coming back. I thought I might die.

The closet was the worst.

No, no, it wasn't.

The worst was feeling him shake me, seeing him standing over me in the darkness.

Get up. Get up.

Dad, Dad, it's the middle of the night.

He'd have the beer smell on him.

I like the night.

Not this time, I'd think, but I'd know what was coming.

A little expedition. Father and son thing. We're going for a drive.

He'd put me in the back seat. We'd go where there weren't any streetlights any longer. Creepy places where it seemed there might be monsters, ghosts.

He'd stop the car. He'd sit there in the front seat with the engine idling.

Maybe this is where we should part company, he'd say to me. I'd be in my pajamas. Sometimes it was winter even. He'd go on talking, drawing it all out.

Maybe this is where I should drop you off.

Talking, talking.
He'd reach for the door handle.

I could you know. I could do it easily. It's only because I'm such a good guy.

All of sudden we'd be out of there. Tires squealing.
Wasn't the end though, was it? Not usually. Sometimes we'd stop a whole bunch of different places. We'd come home really, really late.
Sometimes it was every night. Sometimes months would go by. I never went to bed without thinking about it. I was always afraid.
Thanks, Dad, I had to say, when we got back, before I went to my room. Weird thing was I was sort of thankful.
It's only now I hate him.
Little whiner.
I was eight. Eight.
I didn't have anyone to protect me.
We have come a fair distance. We are on a path but we have gone beyond known territory, beyond where we went yesterday.
Am I still running? Guess I'm not. Guess I couldn't run any longer. Guess I'm walking
Someone must be remembering how to get back again.
Right, oh Ingen, why don't you take care of that? I'm not done. I'm not finished. I have to keep going.
The salt taste's coming back? And the knot in my guts.
But there's nothing to throw up. There isn't. There isn't.
Doesn't matter, does it? Can't fight it.
Got to get down there. Upchuck, upchuck, UPCHUCK.
AGAIN AND AGAIN AND AGAIN.

Five

I THINK YOU SHOULD SIT NOW, REST.

I guess I'm going to have to.

What is this place though?

There would appear to be something in the way of a pit. It has been dug out by someone at sometime. You are upon its edge. You are looking into it.

How can this have happened? I bet there's a whole lot of places I could go on the farm here. So how come I chose this?

Is it that the pit holds memories for you also?

Oh yes, it does.

It's the same shape almost as that toboggan slope I was always trying to get Dad to take me to. Because everyone else went there.

Hell, did I regret it?

Time we went it was so icy everyone else had gone home. We were all by ourselves, and Dad made me keep sliding over and over.

I brought you out here, didn't I?

He pushed the toboggan harder and harder.

Gave up my time for you.

I was going faster and faster every run. There was that bit where it was extra steep. I came off. I hurt myself.

Dad just stood there laughing. He didn't help with the pulling back up either. He stayed waiting at the top.

There was a hedge at the bottom. I kept running into it. That hurt too. Only mostly I wasn't even sorry because no one was supposed to be getting that far. Hedge was the only thing between me and the road.

I wanted to go home. I wanted hot chocolate. Dad made me stay outside.

That'll teach you, he said.

Teach me what? Not to cry when only an idiot wouldn't?

He's such A SHITHEAD. I know that's what he calls me but it's what he is himself.

We are going on, I see.

He's a shithead who…

Once more we are walking. We are heading down the slope.

A shit head who should be in jail.

That's it though, isn't it? Far as I know nothing bad's happening to him. It's me who's always getting punished. How many "foster homes" is it? Frigging PLACEMENTS. Too many to even count. I just know it's been at least one every year. Sometimes two. Sometimes more than that. Some of them I even liked. Didn't last though, did they?

You know also you are throwing stones, don't you?

Yes, actually I do.

I am throwing them at that old car. The one someone's abandoned because they don't want it anymore. The car that's been left there at the bottom.

The car that took people places.

Maybe places where they didn't want to go.

Or maybe the car was the latest thing to brag about.

By an owner who wouldn't spend the money to get new mitts for his kid. When the kid hadn't even lost them. They'd got stolen.

I was teaching you to look out for yourself.

Kid couldn't say though, could he? He couldn't tell the teacher. He had to keep his hands in his pockets. He had to pretend it was his fault he'd left the mitts at home. Lucky she sent him to the lost and found. Might have got frostbite.

An owner who was good at torture.

An owner who could make everything, EVERYTHING, turn out bad.

Like my dad, MY DAD.

Don't cry now, do I? Don't cry ever!

Lots and lots of stones here. Lots and lots and lots.

Car was probably a beauty once. All new and shiny. One of those great big suckers with the fins.

YES! I got the windshield. The windows. Listen. Listen to the smash.

Frig, I wish I had a lighter, matches.

I can just see it. The smoke that'd go up. The flames.

Haven't though, have I? Any ideas, Ingen?

I want no part in this.

You don't, don't you? Something else I've got to take on by myself.

You think I can't do it, do you?

Mr. Goody-Two-Shoes.

You just watch me.

See this? It's a stick. A big stick. A stick that's heavy.

Look at the hood, just look at it. Frigging great dent.

Bet I could pull that door off. Bet if I climbed up on the roof and jumped on it. Bet I could get it to cave in.

Metal, metal, metal! Leap, leap, leap, leap. Crunch, crunch, crunch.

How long have you been here, car? How long have you been slowly rotting?

No more slowly for you, babe. You're getting the full treatment.

You're getting everything I can give.

Six

SHIT, WHAT'VE I DONE?

Gottcha, didn't I?

Hell, yes, he had.

Frigging dad. Frigging father.

I couldn't think, could I? I was just so angry. And now look.

Car's a wreck. But I don't want it to be.

It is a car that was of no use any longer.

Gna, gna, gna, gna, gna, gna.

Frig! Frig! Frig!

It is true there is damage. But I do not believe the damage will matter.

Damage always matters. Damage is stupid. It's horrible. I hate it. I promised myself I wasn't going to do stuff like this. I just wasn't.

I suspect it is likely no one even has to know.

But I'll know. I'll know I lost it. TOTALLY. I'll know I let him win.

And if I could let him win once...who says I won't again? Who says I won't hurt someone sometime?

Wrecked cars in fields are a time-honoured rural custom. You are not the first to have participated in such an activity.

Don't you get it? What other idiots do doesn't matter. It's what I do that counts.

I still do not understand quite. I do not see how your father is winning.
Because it was like it was him inside me. Him getting out.
That is as may be but you cannot go on berating yourself.
Why not? Why shouldn't I? Why shouldn't it scare me shitless? It's the worst. The worst, worst, WORST there is.
It could be that Scott and Jill do not even come here.
Could be they do. And if they do, and they find it's me, I'm just going to be another one of those "bad kids," aren't I? More living, breathing proof of what everyone seems to believe always. It's just not possible. YOU CAN'T BE A FOSTER KID AND BE OK!
Perhaps it would be simplest to own up. You are not the only one in all the world to have been overcome by anger and in your circumstances—
My circumstances? Are you crazy? I'm not telling this to anyone. One more reason to keep my lips zipped. ZZZZT, ZZZZT, ZZZZT, ZZZZT, ZZZZT. After all, if I open them…I don't know now, do I, what might come out?
It is quite some while since you put the stick down.
I didn't put it down. I threw it. I hurled it away from me. I sent it winging.
It is "the quite some while" I am concerned about. First you ran. Now you are merely sitting.
Hoping if I sit long enough, it's all going to look different. Hoping the nightmare's going to go away.
But you need to return. You took off rather suddenly, in difficult circumstances. Scott and Jill will be worried.
Can't afford that, can I?
You also implied you would not be long.
And I haven't been, not really.
Wait. Oh, yes, I have. I'm looking at my watch. I'm seeing lunch must have been hours back. It's afternoon. It's late-ish.
Hell, I'm shaking again. I'm going to have to stop that. I'm at least going to have to get myself on my feet.

Car's like a magnet though. Can't seem to look at anything else.

Perhaps if you would try turning your back.

Perhaps if I would just start moving my sorry ass, you mean? So what, I can still see the wreckage. It's there, at the back of my eyeballs. I'm going to have to get used to that, aren't I?

I would say it will not to be to your advantage to have people come looking for you.

No, it won't.

There is also the Emergency Unit. It can be summoned.

Yes, it can

OK, Ingen, OK. You can get that look off your face. I haven't completely lost my marbles.

I'm off. I'm going. I'm following the track again.

This time somewhat more slowly.

Plod, plod, plod.

Hell, I ran further than I thought. How much land do Scott and Jill have anyway? Maybe I'm lost. Maybe I'm not on the same route after all.

No, no. I can see the cattle. And there's that one with the funny mark on its face. The one Scott called Daisy. They're not just any old cattle then, are they? They're the right ones. Can't believe I just went charging through them. They're pretty big.

They did not, however, harm you.

No, they didn't. Wonder if they ever do anything but eat? And shit. Miracle I didn't step in any of it. Always one of them with its tail up. Soon as that one gets done another starts. Splat, splat, splat. Wouldn't be much of a stretch to think the world could get covered with it.

I believe you are distracting yourself.

But only for a moment. I do know what needs doing. I do know I have to get myself back through that gate. Open AND CLOSE.

Not hard to see why Scott and Jill don't want the cattle out. Imagine the mess.

There they are too—Scott and Jill. I can see them through the window. Scott must be back then.

Little genius.

Shut up, shut up, shut up!

Don't know what to do with this heavy lump I've got inside me. Dull kind of sinking. Feels like it weighs a ton. I need more time to get myself together.

Couldn't I just…

No, I couldn't. Jill's coming out on the porch.

She has been worried. More than she was before even. Lucky I got here.

"Am I glad to see you." Her face is lighting up.

Now's when I really have to look like I'm sorry. Shrug, grin, show…it's sort of a guy thing. I was sort of exploring.

Lots of pats for good old Maeve, wagging her tail like crazy. Giving my hands a lick.

"We were afraid you might have got lost, fallen, broken a leg or something."

All in one piece. Really. See, see, I'm fine.

"Are you sure you're all right?"

Say I try waving my arms, showing some enthusiasm? Say I make like it's all so good out there? Like I got carried away.

Could be Jill's swallowing it.

Sucker.

You really are very inventive.

She's turning, calling through the screen door. "Scott! Scott, he's home."

Guess I only just made it.

"You've been gone so long."

More showing I'm sorry.

"You hardly had any breakfast. You must be hungry."

I can get into that. I can let her know I'm starving, have a grab at my gut.

"At least there's something normal happening! We'll put food first on the agenda." She's moving into get-on-with-it. "Scott's been making soup. He does that when things aren't going too well and where he went today… Let's just say it wasn't quite as jolly as we'd hoped."

That's it? No more crap? No talk of sending me away? Of course, if they knew about…

I'm making my eyes dance. Soup would be good. I'd love it.

"Come on in then."

I'm doing well. Of course there's still Scott to deal with.

He's at the stove, he's wearing his apron again. What's he going to say to me? "I hear you've had some disturbing news."

A nod will do for that one. Is it an opener?

He's letting it lie? He's not saying anything else about it?

Apparently not.

I'll get myself out of the way. I'll show them I need to wash my hands, go to the bathroom. Little one that's downstairs will do fine. Don't know why they didn't tell me about that yesterday, first thing.

Breathe. Breathe.

Sometimes I think bathrooms were invented for escaping to. I can get a drink here. God, I'm thirsty. Water, water.

Turn those taps on. Clean those hands.

Taps off.

Words are coming floating. "Thank heavens he's back, Scott."

"Certainly is a relief. Guess we're just going to have to tread carefully."

Tread carefully? They sound so nice.

Remember? Remember, Jill was angry for you.

Don't know they've got some monster in their midst now, do they?

"He's going to need some looking after."

Makes it even worse.

Unfit for human society you are.

Got that car in my head still, haven't I? Maybe I won't ever be able to get it out.

I wrecked it. I wrecked it. Means I can't trust myself.

Means maybe people aren't safe when I'm around.

I have to keep it a secret too. I can't let anyone know about it.

Secret keeping is hard work.

Too bad, I've got to. I've got to bury it all. Or try to. It's the only thing I can do.

Seven

FRIENDLY, FRIENDLY, FRIENDLY. NICE, NICE, NICE.

I'm not used to it. Not right up against Mr. and Mrs. Household Products. Mr. and Mrs. Don't Drop a Crumb. Makes me feel even weirder.

Here I am, back from the bathroom. Jumpy. Like I'm on pins.

Pins are nothing to what you deserve.

I will deal with him.

I should be chilling out. There's a place set for me at the table. The soup's in a bowl all ready. Only thing I have to do is chow down.

"We need to get something clear."

Oh, oh, Scott. Hate it when people say that.

"This thing with your dad. I gather you don't want to talk about it."

Of course, I don't want to talk about it. I don't even want to think about it. Especially not with them.

"If you don't, we'll do our best to understand." Jill with her two cents. "At least until we have to take some action."

"Whatever has to be decided, we'll decide then."

Frigging hell. They've worked it out. They've set some policy between them. Adults do that.

It is, however, a policy that is in your favour.

Yes, yes, it is.

Can't hardly taste the soup. Think it must be vegetable. Just want to get out of here AGAIN.

What are you? Some kind of loner?

Can't just leave though. Not yet. Too suspicious.

Even if Scott has gone back to the cooking. "Supper. We're having spaghetti. I like a blending of flavours, give it a bit of time."

Shit, Jill's sitting down with me. Wish she wasn't. Wish she wasn't leaning forward, opening her mouth. "In the meanwhile we thought we should fill you in with what's happening on the work front. After all, if you're going to be part of the family you'll need to know this."

A part of the family? I am?

"The thing is we're involved with a wetlands area that's somehow got scheduled for development."

Don't know how to answer.

Probably merely showing concern is all that is required at this point.

Concern, I'm trying for.

"The fact is we got hired to provide the information that would prove how destructive the whole thing will be to wildlife. We thought we had an open and shut case but now there are other forces involved."

"The forces of evil!" Scott's got his arms up. He's making his voice all shivery.

Is he serious or am I supposed to laugh?

There's a mag upside down on the table. I'm reaching towards it, turning it over.

Holy shit. The Himalayas are here too. There are climbers. They're going through some ice field.

"You can borrow that if you're interested." Jill's retreating, pushing her chair back.

I'm flipping the pages. Can't seem to help myself.

"Lots more where that came from," Scott says. "Mountain magazines are our specialty."

I give him a grin. One's enough for now.

"Take, read."

Could that be my cue to be getting myself out of here? Could it? Could it?

Jill's smiling. "It's good to know you share our manias, though why the Children's Aid didn't tell us about what appeals to you I can't imagine."

I shrug. Never got the chance to show anyone before—far as I remember.

Whee-hah! Here I go. I'm putting my bowl and spoon in the dishwasher. I'm hugging the mag more tightly. I'm showing how thrilled to frigging bits I am to be bringing it to my room.

Eight

NIGHT. I CAN'T SLEEP.

Why should you?

Fact is I'm afraid to close my eyes.

In case it's me turns into a werewolf.

It could happen.

In case I wake up and find I've been sleepwalking. I'm doing something terrible. Blood all over

Whole day's with me. Can't stop thinking about it. Pictures keep coming.

Can't stop seeing how Scott and Jill…they got me to come down to lay the table. But they wanted to make supper fun. Scott was doing that stuff with the spaghetti, stringing it out.

And after, they were so pleased I liked the mag. They took me into their office. They showed me pics on the computer. They talked about places they'd been to. They said how once Scott even fell into a crevasse. They told how the guys that were with him had to get him out. They laughed and joked. And they didn't ask about the frigging CAS. Or my dad. They frigging, frigging didn't. Even though I got the feeling Jill wanted to.

She wanted to a lot.

Pair of boneheads. You could rob them blind, they'd never even notice.

I came to bed sort of ok.

As soon as I lay down. As soon as I heard them coming up and going to their room… It's right next door. It's so close to me. Soon as it seemed they weren't talking any longer, they were sleeping, I started being scared.

My legs have these twitches in them. It's like I'm still running.

Bet even Ingen's snoring away by this time.

I certainly am not. How could I be? I am troubled for you. I haven't even put my pajamas on.

What should I do? Can you tell me?

I would suggest you get up.

But I'll wake people.

Not if you go quietly. I am only proposing that you should look out the window.

The window? Oh, that.

Might as well.

Perhaps you will notice it is beautiful out there, in the moonlight.

Perhaps I will.

Big thing I can see really is the barn. That great dark shadow.

Makes me think about the loft.

Shit, there's a lump in my throat.

Loft seems so simple, so easy. So separate.

So like it could be mine.

Nine

"ARE YOU TRYING TO TELL US YOU WANT TO SLEEP ON THAT HAY pile. Here, in the barn?" Jill's asking.

Yeah, yeah, I am.

Why else would I have brought them out here? Why else would I be pointing in the hay pile's direction, putting my hands up to my cheek in that sleep-mime thing?

It is not surprising that they are a little bewildered, however.

Guess it isn't. Seeing as how I did come on them right after breakfast, when they'd hardly finished their coffee. When they were still sipping away.

There I was, in their faces, showing them I wanted them to be following me.

I would say they have been rather good about it all so far.

Whereas you've been more than usually lunatic.

It's not lunatic. It isn't.

Last night, at the window, I sat there and sat there. Everything else went away. I could see myself here. Day after day of it. In the loft. The loft. The only place I've ever wanted to be.

I went back to bed. It was like a dream I couldn't have. I did go to sleep then. I woke up and there was sun on my face. It was morning.

I had this shouting inside me telling me I HAD TO GIVE IT A TRY.

I can't stay in the house any longer. I know I can't. I don't want to. I know I have to be by myself.

Reckon my best chance is to make it all seem like I'm planning sort of an adventure. Something I've never had before. Don't know much about Scott and Jill but I do know adventures turn their crank.

Anyway, it's true. I've never slept out in a tent even and I've always wanted to. I'm not even lying. Not about that.

Trouble is I seem to be pushing the wrong buttons.

"Is there something you don't like about your room? We left it bare specially." There's Jill again, the worrier. A question I hadn't expected.

"Bit sudden, isn't it?" Scott's catching her vibe.

Sudden? Maybe it is. Maybe I should show them I'm a sudden kind of person. Even though I'm not exactly.

Maybe I should have a go at one of my cartwheels. A demonstration of how much I like the space.

Jill's shaking her head. "You, my friend, are a mystery."

Not what I'd have said.

Mystery is good in my opinion. It adds a spice to life.

"I wouldn't blink an eye."

"Not considering the locations we've slept in, Jill-O?"

"It just seems kind of strange though."

Scott's cell is ringing. "I'd better take this."

Jill's pissed off. She's sighing, leaning her ass against the window ledge.

"Yes. Yes. Yes." Scott's saying, shaking his head.

"Never a dull moment is there?" Jill's rolling her eyes.

If I could just let them know. Coming here…I could be saving them from something awful. Can't though, can I? Can't go there.

"Maybe if you hadn't taken off on us. Maybe if you'd let us know how upset this thing with your father has made you."

I was right. She did want more from me yesterday.

Better get back into showing how sorry I am for causing them so much trouble.

You've always been sorry!

Better remind her how I did come back.

"If it was just about your father, I wouldn't be so bothered, but it's been two whole days and you haven't said a thing to us."

Sort of thought they hadn't noticed. Sort of thought they didn't mind.

They should rate themselves lucky. Freed them from your whining.

"There's nothing about not speaking on your records. Not that we were told."

Records? Can't escape them, can I? Stuff that's written about me somewhere. Stuff I never get to read.

"I have to assume it's new. I'm worried it might be something we're doing."

Scott's taken himself off into a corner. Maybe that's lucky. Maybe if he hadn't I'd be dealing with them both.

"You're not a monk, are you? You haven't made a vow of silence?"

That's a good one. A vow of silence is exactly what I've done.

Not going to let her know about that either though, am I? Vows are my own business.

So how am I going to deal with it? Because I'm not giving in.

I think silence is my right. If that's what I want. If that's what I'm choosing. I'll speak when I'm ready. WHEN I FRIGGING DECIDE.

Say I just ignore the whole business. Brush it off.

Go on, walking about here. Spreading my arms out. Making like it's the best place in the world.

Which it is, for me. The best place possible.

I'm excited.

"So sleeping out here is just something you think you'd like to try?"

Lots of nodding for that one. Could be I'm winning her over.

"In half an hour?" Scott's wandering back. He's still talking on his phone. Sure as hell doesn't sound too thrilled.

"As long as it's not because you're unhappy with us," Jill says.

No, no. Couldn't be happier.

"Presumably you're only thinking about one night."

Maybe a couple? Two fingers.

Do not go any further. Do not let them know you're really aiming at moving in.

I'm not brain-dead. I've been finding my way round adults a long, long time.

Scott's closing the phone. He's slipping it into his pocket. "That was John Duncan. He wants to do a conference call in half an hour."

Jill's eyes are going wide. "Half an hour! There's information I'm still looking for."

Scott: "We'd better get going."

So much for me?

That is not the stuff that Scott and Jill are made of.

"It's not fair. I don't think we should leave Kyle hanging."

There you go. There's Jill. I truly do think that at heart she is someone you might trust.

I might, might I? Big thing is Scott looks somehow like he's decided. "He really isn't asking for very much, you know."

Am I glad to hear those words.

"Still." Jill isn't convinced.

Please, please. I've got my hands together. I'm pleading.

Scott has this gleam in his eye. "A room in the stable really. We all know how important that can be."

"All right. All right. We'll go for it."

I am looking as ENTHUSIASTIC as I can get. I'm showing them they won't regret it. Not much time for thanks, they're really in a hurry. They're almost at the ladder. Oh, oh, Jill's stopping.

"We'll go for it but there are a few things we're going to have to give you so we can be sure you're properly taken care of. I insist on that."

Idiots.

Gifts I can handle.

Scott's head is disappearing. "In the meanwhile, enjoy yourself, boy-o. Bring up a couple of things from below maybe. Go the whole hog. Make yourself a real pad."

Ten

WE HAVE MORE IN THE WAY OF COMFORT THAN I HAD ANTICIPATED.

Crates I found mean there's something to sit on.

As I am about to demonstrate.

That long mirror I dug out from under all sorts of everything.

An antique almost.

You wouldn't know an antique if it reared up and bit you.

Looks good in the corner. Classy. An added touch.

Done pretty well for the first day.

Even managed to get my duffle bag over while Scott and Jill were busy. Has my clean clothes in it. I'll need them.

Duffle bag means I have my iPod so I can have some tunes. Not that I've got much of what you'd call a playlist. Mostly I just used it around school so I too could have earbuds in my ears and look cool. Saved up my allowance for it. Seemed important at the time.

There are my bike mags too. And the climbing mag, which I'm still reading.

Kind of wanted to put up my posters. Everest. The Harley. Seemed better to leave them tacked up in my room. So it'd be like for certain I'd be coming back there.

A clever piece of scheming.

You would call it that, now wouldn't you?

I might be anyway, some day.

Who am I kidding? Before that happens I'll have been shipped out. One more reason why I had to get on with this. Had to do it while I could.

Can't believe how Jill was so helpful. She just kept bringing stuff over. Started with a sleeping bag and a sleeping mat. "Better than hay, I assure you."

Then there were those pillows. "I will not have anyone saying we're neglecting you."

Finally it was the flashlights—that honking great monster of a thing and the headlamp. And the bug spray and the water bottle.

By the time I went in for supper she'd worn a path here almost. Scott was suggesting maybe she'd like to add the kitchen sink. He made a joke about it. "We have a nice line in blenders too. We got three last Christmas. We could give you an ice axe so you can fend off marauders."

Jill threw a carrot at him. Scott started chomping on it.

"Lot of help you're being," she told him.

"I have my plans. I intend to add further illumination," he announced.

That's when he gave me the light bulb.

Spoiled brat.

He told me I should put it in that socket, over where the bed is. The socket with the string.

It's like I'm in the lap of luxury. For me anyway. I have everything I need. Totally and utterly everything. And if I just go one day at a time, sort of staying here. Maybe they'll just get used to it. They can't really have set me up with all this for one night, can they?

Think I'll go for a few more cartwheels.

For god's sake!

Even you can't spoil this, Dad.

Didn't hear from good old Wendy again, did I? Maybe the letter thing…maybe it's really, really like you, oh Father. Maybe it's just going to disappear.

Never had a light with a string before.

If you keep flicking it on and off, Scott and Jill might think you are in distress and signalling.

No, they won't. Their lights have gone out. I watched. I saw. Kitchen, living room, upstairs hallway.

They're in bed. They're probably sleeping. Safe, safe, safe.

Splendidly exciting to be the only ones who are awake still, don't you think?

Yeah, I do.

Never had my own PAD before.

Might a small celebration be in order?

Expecting someone to break out a bottle, are you?

No, I'm not.

So is there something you do feel like doing?

Stupid maybe but I feel like going out. I want to go out and be somewhere so I can know I can come back here. I want to go out because no one's watching. Because it's like I'm free.

So why are you hesitating?

It's night.

But nights may be made for walking in. This one is especially auspicious.

Can't hurt, can it? At least I could put on that little headlamp-thingy. I could go down and take a look.

Perhaps some bug spray first?

Bug spray, bug spray. Arms, legs, face, neck.

Better with the headlamp out. Now I'm down here. Now I'm actually standing in the yard.

I can see more. It's not like I'm in a tunnel.

Moon's bigger than it was yesterday even. And if I take one more step I'm where it's brighter. It's like I'm in some golden sea.

How would you know? You've never seen the sea, little shithead.

There are times when restraint grows ever more difficult.

Frig! Look how far my shadow goes.

There's so much quiet. Like I could reach out and take the quiet and hold it. Like I could have it in my hand.

So much for all that whining about being left in dark places, being frightened.

Could be this is DIFFERENT. Shit, it sure, sure could.

Anyway, I'm older.

Big thing is, I've never been less frightened in my life. I should watch out though. Maybe that's because I am now turning into a werewolf. Maybe it's the first sign.

Idea seems kind of funny all of a sudden. Better check though.

No fur on my hands yet. Or my cheeks either. No long ears growing. Don't have an urge to be howling. Toes in my sneakers feel all right.

Here comes Jim-cat! Another night prowler. Definitely off on his own business.

Hell, I'd better be careful. I've forgotten about Maeve. If I make too much noise she might bark. Dogs do that. It's what people have them for.

Jim's disappearing. He's going behind the shed thing.

Great it's so warm. Don't even need a sweater. Good job about the bug spray. Might have had the life sucked out of me without it. Might be turned into a shrivelled husk.

So?

So what?

Come on, Ingen. What's with this hopping from foot to foot, buttoning and unbuttoning your lab coat?

I am hoping this is not the extent of our travels.

All right.

I am wanting to go further.

No problem there. Let's take ourselves through that gate.

How about going over it?

How about just doing that? What about a bit of balancing? Standing? Leaping off the top like Batman, cape all flying. Superman. Awesome. Who's the hero? SHAZZAM, SHAAAAZZAAAM.

Cattle aren't even around. Must've wandered off. Scott said they do that sometimes. Scott's big on cattle. Another thing I've found out.

So the world is our oyster.

It is. The dark's making a space for us almost.

This has to be the stupidest idea you've come up with yet.

You do not have to accompany us.

Count me out then.

Count him out! That's really something.

An achievement.

Finding where my dear old daddy will not go.

Moonlight's amazing. Never thought about it before, how the moonlight really does let you see. It lets you see but it makes everything different. Blocks and shapes and stuff.

Winter-shelter barn on the right. Winter-shelter barn looming. Winter-shelter barn passed.

We are stopped.

The field's so big. I have to get used to how it all is. I've never been out on my own in the night like this before.

Adults don't exactly go for it. They want you where they can see you.

Adults! Adults! Scott and Jill. They wouldn't like this, would they? Jill especially.

They didn't say I couldn't though, did they? Probably because they didn't even think about it.

We all of us need our own endeavours.

Another secret? If I've got one, I might as well have another. This one's good though. Good, good, GOOD.

OK. OK. I'm feeling with my feet how the track is. How it's not the same as the grass. The grass is softer, more springy.

The grass. The grass.

The grass is shining almost. I've truly never seen anything like it. Stretching and stretching. On and on. On is where I want to go too. On and on forever.

Except…had to happen, didn't it? We're nearly at the frigging pit.

If I don't look…

The pit is full of shadows.

The shadows are deep. I can't see ANYTHING.

Now there are trees. Track goes between them. World's darker here. It smells damper. Trees make everything a bit more scary. Really is more difficult to find my way. Should I turn back?

Do you want to?

No, no. I can manage. I just have to work harder. It's still all right though. I still only need the flashlight now and then.

There's this little breeze coming. The patterns the tree-shadows make on the ground are changing from the movement of the leaves. I can hear something too. Sounds like water. Sounds like a stream.

A stream. Yes. Kind of gurgling.

Bet I could cross it if I stepped on those stones.

One….two….three….and four. Didn't even get my feet wet. How about a couple of Tarzan chest beats? Got to do something to celebrate my success.

Thanks, Ingen. Thanks for the bow. I like that.

The track's still there. It's going up a little slope. There are roots to watch out for. More trees crowding.

Holy, moly. I'm in this bowl place. The grass is longer. It's rougher. It's brushing against my jeans. Openness means everything's all bright again. And the track does STILL go on.

Get a load of those bushes. Hair like witches. Could be a perfect place for a werewolf gathering, couldn't it?

If that is what you want.

Why would I? Why would I want anyone else here, let alone a horde?

It'd be awful. There'd be so much noise.

Why do I have this werewolf obsession anyway? What's with it? Should forget it.

You have stopped again.

I've stopped to give myself a moment to drink it in. It's weird. The further I go, the more I feel I belong here. Like the quiet's coming in me. Like I'm safe.

We are off once more then?

We're off for certain. We're going to the right.

It delights me that you can appreciate this.

Appreciate it? I love it.

Guess those trees there must be birches.

The ones with the white bark?

Track's going up again. Not very much though. I've come to another flat place. Only it isn't flat for long. We're going down.

There's water, but it's not moving. The trail's stopped. It's ended. I'm by this lake.

A lake that's not like any lake I've ever seen before. There are dead trees coming up out of it. The trees are standing still, and… stark. Not one of my usual words. Only one that seems to fit though because the branches are all bare.

I think it should be ugly, but it isn't.

It's eerie. There's a smell to it. Kind of misty, kind of smoky, almost catching in my throat.

It isn't ugly, it's wonderful. There are fireflies even. Not on the water, along the shore.

The moon's making a path. Not a path I could walk on, of course. The path's on the water.

Maybe if I was someone else, I'd think it was nothing. But I'm not anyone else and I'm not with anyone. There's just me and it.

And me, of course/

Of course, Ingen. But you're a part of who I am. You said that. You told me.

Guess it isn't quite what you'd call a lake, not really. Guess it's more of a swamp. Looks like something happened here. Long ago maybe. Something to make it how it is.

Doesn't matter how it came. It's a swamp where I am. A swamp where I'm sitting. Where I've come through the nighttime to be.

Eleven

"KYLE!"

Someone's calling your name, oh shithead.

Someone? Scott!

OK. So I'm getting my eyes open.

Hell it's bright. Bright daylight. Too bright. Loft's all sunshine.

I should've been up early. I should have been doing something about all those fears and suspicions Scott and Jill must have about me. Proving there isn't really anything weird about wanting to sleep in a barn.

Better get myself up and at 'em quickly.

"Kyle! Kyle!"

They cannot, cannot, CANNOT have a clue I've been tromping about in the dark.

Shit, it's almost noon.

Hardly surprising, of course, time I got back. How long did I stay on that rock there? It was all so amazing. Moon was going down for certain. Moon was what got me moving. Didn't think I could manage in the absolute dark.

"Kyle! Kyle!" Scott's voice is getting louder. Seems like he'll be here any minute. I've got to stop letting the moonlight fill my brain.

I have to drag myself up, show my face, look down the ladder.

"Ah, alive and well, I gather." Scott is grinning. He's also coming up.

I'm scratching my head and yawning, letting him know there's nothing wrong. There isn't really. I'm a teenager. Teenagers are famous for late mornings.

Funny how pleased he looks. Like he really does quite like me being in this place.

Wonder why he hasn't come right up? Why he's stopped a few steps down.

"I was toiling away, nose to the grindstone." He's so joke-y. "Came to me I hadn't seen hide nor hair of you. I had this feeling I should come and make sure you're still in the land of the living."

Land of the living? Ta, da! Ta, da!

Maybe if he's just come to check, he'll go away again. Wouldn't be bad that, getting back into the sleeping bag, catching a few more zees.

"Anyway, I thought you might like an outing."

Shit. More zees cancelled. I'll have to go, won't I? I'll have to look willing. Big thing is not to let him see how tired I am. "Outing," sounds ominous. Almost like my dad. Not that we ever went in daytime.

Scott still isn't coming up here, not climbing those last few steps. I'm only getting the top half of him. Looks kind of funny. "I've had a call from the Bird Rescue Centre."

So there's a destination. We're not just going wandering about. Not that I actually know what a Bird Rescue Centre is, of course.

The name may tell you all, in fact.

Ingen, buddy! Awake at last!

Scott's going on. "I suppose it's one more thing you need to know about us. We sometimes take in orphans."

Orphans? There *are* other kids coming then?

Get with it, dough-head.

You must attend. You must listen.

"They've got one now they want us to pick up."

Who does?

The Bird Rescue Centre.

An orphan bird then. That's a new one. If I didn't have fur on my tongue from not sleeping enough, this whole thing might be going better. There's sand too, under my eyelids. Still, the info is apparently going to keep coming. Feels like Scott's on a roll. "I usually leave it to Jill. It's more her baby. It's her that's at the meeting this time though."

Nod once, twice, to show I'm keeping up with it all.

"We're trying to spread the load so we're not both out together, leaving you alone here, although it's probably going to have to happen before too long."

Happy little shrug to show alone would be fine. Not too much enthusiasm though. In case he thinks I'm waiting to burn the place down.

What an adventure we had last night. How simply splendid.

Bird Rescue Centre! I told you these people were dummies.

OK, guys, I'm busy. Could you keep it down?

Scott's getting to the point. "We need to hop to it."

I'm giving him a smile to show "hopping to it" is right up there with what I'm planning. Lucky I went to bed with my clothes on. One less task to carry out. Would there be time for something to eat though maybe? Breakfast?

"I suppose we might allow it. We're really not in the business of starving you."

We're off to the kitchen. I'm grabbing some OJ. I'm hitting the bathroom. I'm splashing water on my face. The sand is a little bit less now. Better clean those teeth.

"How about cereal?"

Yeah, yeah. I'd like that.

"Corn flakes?"

Corn flakes would be great.

"Ready?"

Don't think I'd go as far as that quite. Still I can manage to get myself into the car. Scott's car. The car that isn't smashed up, broken.

Do not go there.

No, no, no. DO NOT. Focus on how the car is sort of in the same state as the house. How can people have so many books and papers?

I was planning to catch another forty winks in the back here.

Wish I could do the same. Being in the car means I'm a prisoner.

Scott's showing me the sights. "Our property ends at that fence line."

I have to keep looking like I care. Of course, if I could drive myself, whole thing would be different. Car's not as good as a Harley. Almost though.

"This is our nearest village."

Why do I have to bother, considering I'm only going to be living here ten minutes? Or so it will seem.

"It's not much of a place, not really."

I can see that but I don't think I should show it. Always better to aim for positive. People are weird about their neighbourhoods, I've found.

"We have to go into the city if we want to do any real shopping. Grocery store here's about as close to a convenience store as you can get."

He's right about the "grocery store." Smallest one I've ever seen. That's it? The village is done?

"These woods are among my favourites. I love the maples."

Yadda, yadda, yadda. Wish we could get this over with.

I offered to set you free from the car so often. So how come you weren't grateful?

Yeah! How come?

Can't I go to sleep, just for a little?

"This thing with the Bird Centre…"

No, I can't.

"Jill's been volunteering there for ages."

Sounds like we're getting onto some other track, something that might explain some stuff.

"Jill's into the rescuing business."

Got it! Got it. Why I'm here. Always good to know that. Although rescuers are tricky. They get disappointed so easily.

"I'm the one said we should quit with the animals and get into people though."

People? I'm on the to-do list?

You are so cynical.

So would you be. Still, I'm glad you're awake again. You can help me out.

"Not that Jill wasn't for it."

Looks like I'm getting the full story.

"We'd actually been talking about it for ages. It was always something we planned to do. I had this brother. He kind of got lost when we were teenagers. He was killed in an accident."

Holy shit! How am I supposed to respond to that?

"He was into more bad stuff than I care to mention. Drugs probably weren't even the half of it."

I could've told you there was something here didn't smell right.

Scott's staring ahead of him. "I always thought he might've got out of it if I'd helped him more. I wasn't very old myself though."

Scott's swallowing. He's swallowing hard.

Get it! Scott had a brother who was a druggie.

I'm way, way out of my depth.

"I do know you're not his replacement."

Maybe I should try the staring ahead thing. Can't think of anything else.

"You're not even like him."

Am I supposed to be grateful for this wondrous piece of knowledge?

"From what we heard, your behaviour is almost impeccable, even if you do have this odd quirk about sleeping arrangements."

OK, we're back to the joking. Could be safer.

"There is, of course, also your penchant for silence."

Or not safer after all. What is it with not-speaking? Why are people so bothered? Why isn't it OK to make up my own mind? Didn't we have some unit in frigging social studies on choices? So, I'm choosing. Wonder if Jill's set him up for this? Wonder if he actually cares?

Thank frig. There's a sign. The words say Harrington's Bird Rescue Centre. They say it in big red letters. Rescue is in sight.

And you hardly needed me at all. You should remember that.

Maybe I did, maybe I didn't. Anyway, I was right. We've arrived. Scott is pulling into the Rescue Centre driveway. Scott is getting out.

Another opportunity for the exploration of new territory.

I am onto it. Fact one: there's a house. Fact two: the house has a tall, high gate beside it. Fact three: the gate has a bell to push and a sign that says "For the Centre, please ring here." Nothing too difficult.

Scott's got the bell pressed. The gate is opening. A woman is appearing. Seems kind of animal keeper-y.

Animal keeper-y is not a term I have heard before.

That's because I made it up. Only thing seems to fit her.

Skirt dragging round her ankles. Looks like she's been pulled through a bush.

How unfortunate that your father decided on this occasion he should join us.

Probably should haul myself out.

Here we go.

"Scott! Scott! I am glad to see you."

The preliminaries: "Jill's not home yet. I brought Kyle instead."

"And Kyle is…?"

Kyle is into the hello-nod.

I told you nods are useful.

"Kyle is a young man who's come to live with us. Kyle, meet Tanya. Tanya, meet Kyle."

Come to live with them? Kind of like that. Sounds better than "foster" whatever. Way better than CAS deportee.

Tanya's putting her hand out so I can shake it. She's a bit too eager, too friendly.

She's a bird nut.

Tanya is welcoming us into her yard. Holy shit, there are cages all over.

This is the closest thing to a zoo I have visited in quite some while.

Stupid do-gooders.

No lions or tigers, however.

No, there are not lions or tigers. Birds are apparently where it's at. Feels like everything's all filled with fluttering and tweeting. I've never seen so many birds in my whole life. Cages are filled with branches and perches and feeders. Birds are flying about inside. Although not all of them.

Scott's going over to a cage where there's a speckled-y bird that's pecking about on the ground. "I'm attached to this little grouse guy. His name's Charlie."

Tanya doesn't seem so happy about him. "Charlie's been here so long, he's almost part of the family." She has something she wants to tell me. "We try to get them back into the wild, Kyle, but Charlie's wing never healed right."

Meaning? Charlie is grounded FOR LIFE.

Wish she hadn't told me. Wish I didn't know.

Scott's pretty eager. "Where's our new charge then?"

Tanya's going to this little wooden building. "She's in the feed shed."

We are following along. Feed shed is filled with plastic garbage cans with labels on. We're heading towards the back where there's a cage on a counter. A small cage, more rickety.

"She got dumped off this morning."

A cage with a bird that looks like a crow. Yeah, it's a crow, I'm sure of it. Aren't crows supposed to be bigger though? Aren't they supposed to sort of strut?

Tanya's shaking her head. "As you can see, she's quite young."

I guess that explains the size thing.

Doesn't explain why she's huddling into herself, like she's trying to disappear. Why the moment Scott takes a step nearer she does what she can to back up. When she's in the corner already. When she has nowhere else to go.

Tanya's into giving us all the info. "I left her in her own cage because I didn't want to scare her any more than I had to. I thought you could take her in it. That way the journey will be the least disruption for her."

Big thing I want to know is how she got here. She can't have walked, can she?

"I have no idea who brought her. I just know they came in a truck. I heard it but by the time I got to the gate the truck was disappearing."

That's it, isn't it? She was dumped off, she was left, she was abandoned, she was on a doorstep like I was. She's frightened. Frightened as hell. I know what I'd do if I could. I'd pick her up. I'd hold her. I'd tell her everything'll be all right.

It'd make it worse though, wouldn't it? Just touching her. Who am I to say it'll be all right anyway? Who am I to promise that?

"We're full up and fit to bust. We don't have any room for her."

Where have I heard that one?

Can't we get on with this? Can't we get her out of here?

"The vet's seen her, of course?" Scott has his own questions. Details, details.

Tanya's right onto it. "I got him straight away."

Surely a bird should move? Surely it shouldn't just sit there?

"And he said…?"

Come on, Scott, leave it. We know all we need to.

"He said she wants feeding up, with a proper diet."

"That we can manage."

That, I am glad to hear. So why aren't we going?

"There's more."

I don't want any more but it looks like we're going to get it.

"Her pin feathers have been clipped so she can't fly. That's no big deal, they'll grow back again. The worst is her tongue's been split."

Scott's face is really angry now. "What the hell for?"

Do I want to know? Do I?

"Whoever had her wanted to teach her to talk. There's an old rural belief that says tongue-splitting will make it more likely."

"It's bloody barbaric."

"It is, but it happens."

Little crow, what have they done to you? Little crow, little crow, little crow.

Twelve

NO USE FOR ME ANY LONGER, IS THERE?

Jill got here ahead of us. Scott called her on the cell. He told her she should get home quickly if she could. And she did. She was waiting for us. She's better than me too. She's holding her bit of the cage steadier.

I was so nervous when we were getting out of the Centre, Scott and me together. When I had one end of the cage and he had the other. All I could think of was how every little movement made the crow look more terrified than she had before.

Ride here was horrible. Crow was on the back seat.

I kept seeing what it must have been like, having the scissors coming at her. And after. Like it was me. Even Scott was quiet. Maybe he was thinking the same thing.

Two of them sure are a team. They move like one person almost. They seem to have almost the same thoughts.

Jill is right at it too.

All too eager!

She'd opened the car door before we'd hardly stopped. She'd got everything set up for us. "I cleared that space on the porch we use always." That's what she said.

They have done this before, of course.

Scott didn't have to tell her anything. Jill was all over it.

Bleeding-heart-er.

She's so efficient. Listen to her. "I dug out the special chow. I bet she's dehydrated."

Shouldn't they have something better to do with themselves?

What's it to you, DADDY? Don't you get it? There's something hurting. Hurting badly. You wouldn't get it, would you? You'd probably be a tongue-splitter yourself. You can shut the crap up. I like it that Scott and Jill are doing what they're doing. I like it a lot.

You're as bad as they are.

Yeah I am. And I'm proud of it.

Right, right, they're across the yard.

Don't seem to worry about Maeve fussing around, do they? *No doubt she also has been down this road on other occasions.*

They're going up the steps. They've almost got the cage in place. One, two.

Jill: "OK, OK. Let's get her lowered."

Scott: "The blocks need moving just a little."

Jill: "I'm onto it."

That's it. It's done.

Scott's got his arm around Jill's shoulders. They're standing together like when I first came here.

"It's all right, little one. It's over. No more moving," Jill's saying.

I feel so stupid, hanging about. Maybe, I don't have to stay here. Maybe, now they've got the cage settled I can take myself away. They're hardly even noticing me any more anyway.

Wrong on that one. Jill's got me in her sights again. "You can go and get yourself some lunch if you want, Kyle."

I don't think I'm up to lunch. Not with what's happening. Fact is I've never been less hungry in my life.

Didn't occur to me the crow could look more pathetic. She does though. Her head's so squashed down, her neck's gone almost. Her feathers are like they're drooping.

"Barbaric" is what Scott called what's been done to her, isn't it?

Barbaric and meals don't go together. Not for me.

I'm going with Plan A—getting out of here. I'm pointing, indicating.

"Back to the barn, is it?" Scott's asking.

Yes, yes, it is.

I just don't want to look at her any more.

I wouldn't. Except the loft has its frigging window.

So, guess what? I've climbed the ladder. I've given up on the idea of lying down on the bed again. I'm at the window. I'm staring out.

Scott and Jill are still there. They're talking to one another. I can just catch what they're saying.

"She's really young. Did they steal her out of the nest, do you think?" Here come Jill's questions.

Shit, Scott's going to have to go over all the gory details, repeat them. I know I don't have to listen. I know if I don't drag myself away I will.

You could take another walk.

Doesn't seem right somehow. Going off into the distance. Don't know why.

Perhaps then you will simply have to opt for activity.

Push-ups? Knee-bends? Certainly not into cartwheels.

I was thinking rather of seeing if there are further improvements we can make to our abode.

What sort of improvements?

We could return below. We could consider whether there is anything further we are needing. We would be in the vicinity but our minds would be occupied, at least partially.

Yeah, yeah. Why not? Scott and Jill are going in now anyway. Isn't anything else going to happen. Not just yet.

Down I go again then. Down, down, down.

Suppose I could have a sit on the tractor, pretend I'm driving it.

Like some three-year-old!

Seat's the pits. Bare metal with this skinny little cushion. Probably should get off.

Fact is I've looked here already. I'm pretty clear about how I don't need one of those great long saws. I don't need a rake with a broken handle, or a bench even. I certainly don't want a dresser in some sick-pink colour. I do not need a baby carriage with its hood gone. Or a stroller with a wheel off.

Mostly I don't want the loft all cluttered.

There are, however, the contents of those shelves.

It's just a bunch of cans.

Cans of paint, I believe.

What am I going to do with that?

Paint is, I think, customarily used for painting.

Dummy.

Most people put paint on their walls.

But there's only black.

Even black may find its true location.

Black drives adults crazy. You should've seen what happened to that kid in school last year that fixed his room up while his parents were away. He got kicked out. They called in counsellors and everything

Do you wish to drive anyone crazy?

Of course not! Haven't I said that? Trouble's not my bag.

Nevertheless we might still consider the other possibilities.

You're pretty determined, aren't you? All right then, if it's going to make you happy, I will bring a couple of cans upstairs. I will set them in the middle of the floor and I will agree to think about them. Satisfied, oh Lord of Ingenuity?

Most satisfied, thank you.

Frig, now I'm here, I'm going to have to go back to the window.

Soft-hearted sucker.

Little crow, you aren't exactly chowing anything down yet, are you? You're still in that corner.

Wonder if I looked as shit-scared as you do? When I was at the police station. When I was crying. When the snot was coming out of my nose. Someone gave me a Kleenex. Felt like I needed a whole box.

Good thing I learned to tough it out better. Should've done that sooner, when I was still with my dad.

Sit up, little crow. You'll feel better. At least have something to drink. Drinking's important. Drinking matters.

She is still so new here.

Maybe I will give myself a stretch out, on the sleeping bag. Maybe I'll just do that. Head back. Eyes closed. Think, think, think.

Of what?

Something good. Something distracting. Something like… Last night. Trees, moonlight. Wish I'd had a camera.

A camera is only one method of capturing an image. There are others.

Such as, buddy?

Such as through the use of that which you have recently acquired, for instance.

He's talking about the paint, dork.

Paint does not simply have to cover walls. Paint can be used to make pictures.

Get real! I've never "painted" anything. Not so it looked like it was supposed to.

There is always a first time.

Art class is the worst. Makes me feel stupid, frigging hopeless.

But you are not in art class.

I'm not. And I'm not having anything to do with whatever it is you're suggesting. I'm not going to mess this place up. I'd rather…. Hell, I'd rather just go and have a look at the crow again. I'd rather get on with checking her out one more time.

Thirteen

"NOT EXACTLY IMPROVING, IS SHE?"

Here we are, me and Jill. We're on the porch. Where I've been a lot. Ever since the crow first got here.

Three days it's been. Three days of her just sitting there, huddling. Three days of her not eating or drinking anything at all. I was sure she'd just start into it. She hasn't.

"I find it so hard to leave her."

I know that one.

Little idiot, how many hours have you spent here?

Keep thinking if I stay a bit longer surely she'll have to at least lift her head. Though what I'll do if she does I don't know. I'll see it though, won't I?

Jill's into chatting. "It was good of you to go into the garden and dig those worms for her."

Why wouldn't I?

Seeing as how she and Scott had said at lunchtime that live food might help her. Seemed the least I could do was give it a try.

Digging the worms was the easy part, putting them in that tub thing. Hard part was opening the cage, having her look at me like I'm some kind of monster. Only one she doesn't seem to mind is Maeve. Maeve puts her nose close to the wire quite often. Maeve's the guardian. Herds old Jim-cat off.

Three days. I would not have thought a bird so young could have gone so long without sustenance.

Neither would I. Worms were nice and fresh when I got them. Now they're all shrivelled and awful.

Scott and Jill have tried everything. Cookies even, because Scott said although cookies aren't good for her they might be what she's used to. They might "trigger her eating reflexes." That means start her doing what she should be when it comes to getting stuff down.

Cookies, worms, bird chow, lettuce. It's like she's forgotten what food is. Water too. There's this little drink do-hickey. She's not using it.

Come on, little crow. Come on.

Oh, oh. Seems like Jill's got something she wants to tell me. She's doing the Jill-fidget. "You should know, it's not looking very hopeful."

What does that mean?

What does it sound like, dumbo?

"I know you're not going to want to hear this but the fact is sometimes they just give up. Nobody knows why. We do our best. We do our best always. Sometimes it's just not enough. We come out. They're dead. There's nothing we can do about it. You should be prepared for that. It'll help you."

Help me? How can it? Anyway, I'm not what counts. It's her— it's the crow that needs helping. Didn't occur to me…. She can't be going to die. I've been planning for her. I've been watching all the other birds around here. I've been seeing them up there, in the sky. I've been picturing her.

Tanya said her pinfeathers didn't matter.

She did also say—

I know. I haven't forgotten about her tongue. But things heal. Her tongue's going to have to stop hurting eventually, whatever's been done to it.

Birds have hugely high metabolisms.

Scientific bullshit.

Birds must eat all the time.

"Kyle…Kyle, I'm sorry." Jill's got her hand on my arm. I'm not sure about that, having her touch me. Not much I can do about it right now though. "I just don't think she can last out much longer." Jill's looking so sad.

It may be also that the crow is in shock.

Little crow, you've got to go on living. You've got to.

Who says so?

I do.

Who d'you think you are then?

Jill's standing up. She's looking down on me. "I suppose I'll have go back to work. There's enough of it. We thought the summer would be slack. Turns out it isn't. We're leaving you to your own devices a helluva lot more than we planned to."

Still kind of nervous about letting her know this really, really is all right. More than all right. If it wasn't for the crow, I'd be in heaven. Hours and hours of not having my life all mapped out for me is suiting me just fine. I can even be bored if I want to. Not that I am. I've never been less bored ever.

It's so good being freer. Deciding things.

Loft's a wonder. And I love it, taking off for walks, seeing how things are growing, even yesterday when it rained so suddenly, when I got sopping. Nights are the best of course, although the moon's getting smaller. I may have to give up on that before too long.

And the car you wrecked?

All right, the car I wrecked. Thing is the car isn't going anywhere. Like it or not, it's something I have to look at now and then. When I look I remember. I remember and that's that.

Wish Jill would go in. I know why she hasn't, of course. It's like she said. Getting out of here is hard. Her hand is on the door handle at last though. "I guess I'm going to have to bite the bullet."

She's gone. No, she's come back. But it's only been a minute. "Hey, I forgot. Scott sent you a message. He said to ask you if you're up for another tractor lesson this evening?"

RIGHT ON.

"Seems as if you did pretty well yesterday."

Maybe I did.

Maybe you didn't.

Wasn't something I was expecting. There I was in the bottom of the barn with Scott, because he wanted me to help him look for some special hammer. All of a sudden, he was slapping the tractor's hood. "Fancy a ride?" he said to me.

I nodded.

Enthusiastically.

He backed the tractor out and we were off. Never entered my head once we got to the fields he'd start letting me learn how to drive it. And he's such a good teacher. He set it all up. He showed me how to do that thing with the clutch. Easing it off so I could actually get her moving. He laughed when I did it too quickly. He said that's what everybody does at first.

That is as may be. I believe Jill is waiting for an answer.

So, she is. Whoop-dee-do. I am showing MY ENTHUSIASM again.

"Good. I'll tell him. He'll be pleased."

Oh, will he?

"Now I really am returning to my computer."

I should go and practise. I should get myself ready.

Leave your precious orphaned creature?

Little crow, I'm sorry. Maeve'll be with you though. Little crow, come on. Come on. You're safe here. You are really.

If you are going....

If I'm going, I should walk across the yard. I should go round all the junk in the barn's bottom. I should put my foot on the tractor step, pull myself up.

Seat's still harder than hell. So what? If Scott can stand it, I can.

OK, foot on the clutch. That's the first thing, isn't it? Gearshift goes forward to get into first. Comes back into second, goes up and across into third.

It's all so stiff. Scott said that. He said it's because the tractor's old. He also said it's not like a car. You don't shift gears when you're moving. There's two sets of brakes and there's no gas pedal. Well, there is, sort of but it's called a throttle and it's kind of awkward. He said the throttle's for the next lesson. I guess that means today.

Good to have a look at where everything is. Levers, pedals. Can't really do much though, not without getting her moving.

Thinking of taking her for a spin then, are you?

There aren't any keys.

Say there were.

If there were, I wouldn't use them. I'm not like you. I'm not. I made one mistake. I'm not making another. Not that sort anyway. I'm not stealing, taking stuff that isn't mine.

Good lad. I knew you could be counted on.

Have to admit, without the keys, there's nothing else I can do. But I can't go back to the porch again. Not just yet.

Boom box Scott and Jill have given me is awesome. Ancient as all get-out, but amazing. Specially if I use the 'phones so I don't have to fill the whole world with the noise of it, just me.

Boom box it is then. Music time. Up into my nest again. Back in my own abode.

What'll it be? Something from the CDs Scott and Jill said I could plunder? Some group I've never heard of? How about Johnny Rotten and the Sex Pistols? Sounds promising. I could even do some air band. Use the mirror to watch myself. Try some dancing.

In case you ever get invited to a party?

Because I frigging feel like it, all right?

Even I think you might need to engage in something with more sense of purpose.

Ingen, Ingen, Ingen! Still concerned about those paint cans, are we? Right now I'm thinking of using them as platform-boot look-alikes, give myself a bit of height.

That would seem to me to involve a case of wasted opportunities.

I'll take the goddamn cans back down, put them on the shelves again, if you don't quit nagging me. I didn't get you here for that.

But you have to admit....

OK, OK, I am turning down the music. I am facing it. It is all in my head still. I don't even have to go to the swamp any longer. I keep seeing it. Trees, moonlight. How it'd look on the wall there. How I'd make it really, really big. The idea of it. The excitement.

Now we are talking.

But say I mess up?

You can paint what you do not like over. A black wall will not be so terrible. It might even be a good setting for your posters—Everest, the Harley.

Ingen, don't tempt me.

Why should I not?

Because...because...

Because I don't actually have any rollers or brushes. I don't have the tools I would need.

Oh, come along. Kyle, you are a man of imagination. I have every confidence that you can find a solution to a problem of such stunning simplicity, especially in this environment.

I do have a solution, don't I? I can see that too in my mind.

Fourteen

HELL, WHAT AM I DOING, HANGING ABOUT AT THE BOTTOM OF the painting ladder, not climbing up? Why am I so scared?

I've taken the paint can up. I've hung it on the S hook. I have the paintbrush in one of my hands even. I know about paint too, don't I?

That place before Mr. and Mrs. Household Products. Guy was always into "decorating." One job after another. Treated me like his slave.

I know paint has to be stirred and I've stirred it.

Maybe, for once, you'd rather not make a prize idiot of yourself.

I've done what has to be done. I've got all the stuff together. Wasn't even that difficult. I just took one of the paint cans to Scott and Jill in their office. I showed how I wanted to dip in a brush and get it doing what brushes do.

Jill put up a bit of a fight, of course. Jill's the tough one. She came at me with how I'm really settling in, in the loft here. I'm not planning on coming back to the house at all.

Which is, of course, the truth.

Trouble was she seemed hurt about it. Hadn't thought of that. I had to show how I love going over for meals, and showers, and whatever.

"Using the house as a hotel?" was what she said to me.

I didn't know what to do. It was Scott who saved me. He's so easy. He made this silly little bow.

"Fear not," he said to her. "If all else fails, I shall entice the man forth with the tractor. He shall not be remote from us."

Jill caved pretty quickly after that. Scott swept me off to the basement. He told me I should take whatever I wanted. Paint thinner, rags, stir stick, "the whole shooting match."

Guess I should be grateful to the decorating man. Pete, was it? Guess without him I wouldn't have known about all that.

Jill's so funny too. When we went back up it was her said about how I was going to need this ladder. It was her went and found it where they'd put it in the shed. "Witness to the fact we have not been doing much reno of late."

She sent Scott off to help me get the ladder up here too.

Neither of them even looked to see what colour the paint is. Neither of them seemed to care.

Wouldn't have been able to do much without the ladder, would I? Don't know why I didn't think of that.

"Have a good time," Scott said when he left me. He's into good times it seems. Or maybe it's just they're so busy. They're just happy to have me AMUSED.

Wonder what they'd say if they knew I'm planning on some picture? One more secret. Never had so many in my life.

Maybe that's not true. Never told anyone about my dad, now did I? Not what he did to me. Didn't want anyone to know.

But this is different. Really, really different.

It's secrets I'm glad to have.

Including the car, would you say?

Of course not, the car. Why are you always on about it? Can't you leave it alone?

Big thing right this minute is I'm ready. I can see the crow too, out the window. I can watch her, now and then. Case she needs me. Not that it's the window wall I'm working on. It's the one on the opposite side from my bed.

I'm ready.

Trees, moonlight. I know what they look like.

My son, the artist.

I just feel kind of nervous.

It is a big undertaking.

Waste of good paint.

It is important to you. You care about it.

Guess I do. I actually care a lot.

Artists are always nervous.

I'm not an artist. I'm just making a picture.

Whether you are or you aren't it would be better to get on with it. Supper will come soon and after supper there will be more tractoring. Scott has insisted upon it.

I could wait till tomorrow.

I do not think that would be advisable.

Maybe if I could get the first line done. Maybe if I went up there… Trees are straight, aren't they?

Done it. Made the climb.

I'm up. I'm ready. I'm where the paint can is.

So, say I just start walking downwards, with the paint-filled brush against the wall. Yes, yes. It's making a mark. Kind of thin at the bottom where the paint's almost run out. I can see it though.

I'm going back again. I'm making another line—to the right, with a bit of a curve at the top for one of the branches. And lines in the middle, at the top, for where the branch divides.

Shape seems OK. It does really.

So if I fill the space in between…

You'll be colouring. Just like kindergarten!

You can call it what you like, Dad, but you can't stop me. I'm into it. I frigging, frigging AM.

Fifteen

PAINT, PAINT, PAINT.

That's it. The first tree's finished. One coat anyway. Is it all right?

Hours I've been at it. Couldn't get that much done before supper. Came right back after the tractor lesson. Couldn't wait.

Checking it out makes me nervous again. I'm tingling all over. So hard to tell, isn't it? I need to stand back a bit.

How far would you like to be going?

Or maybe I need to not see it for a while.

You could try turning the light off.

Guess I could. I could try shining the flashlight—the big one. Making it like the moon. Course I can't have it on the water. Haven't done the water yet. Don't even know how I'm going to.

There it is though. That's a tree all right. A big tree. Like I wanted. Bare. At the front, in the centre, where I imagined it. Branch I put in is perfect. Reaching up and out, making a sort of a split. There are going to be other trees of course.

I would sincerely hope so.

I can see where they'll go too. Tomorrow's when I'll start on them. Except….say I just did one more outline.

I, for one, am tired.

Tired doesn't exactly describe it. More like exhausted. Couldn't actually hold the paintbrush much longer, arm is aching so much.

But I'm so pumped.
The morning truly will come, you know.
OK, oh weary, weary scientist. Let's rest our weary heads.

Sixteen

LITTLE CROW! LITTLE CROW!

It is hardly light. The dawn has not even broken.

Doesn't matter. I was dreaming about her. She was how I'd thought about her. She was flying away. She was up in the sky.

A good sign, perhaps?

Might be. How do I know? Might mean she's gone to the great crow heaven. I've got to go and look. Not through the window. Can't see well enough. I've got to get down there.

Whole thing's ridiculous. I'm not going anywhere.

Why should I care?

Fourth day now, isn't it? Jill said three days were too much for her. Still I'm coming gently. Don't want to startle her.

Frig! She's got her eyes closed.

That is after all what things do when they are sleeping.

What if sleep isn't what this is?

If you would look more carefully, you would see that she is breathing.

Guess she is.

I would suggest that you should leave her resting. I would suggest we should return to resting ourselves.

Are you kidding? I'm up. I might be able to do that other tree outline now, before breakfast. And I can do some planning, figuring. How it's all going to be.

You go back to sleep again if you want to. I've got stuff I want to get done.

Seventeen

"DO I GET A SNEAK PREVIEW?"

What got into me? Why am I standing at the window? Why did I choose this moment to be looking out?

You heard Jill calling to Scott, telling him she was going to the mailbox, which is at the end of the laneway.

So?

You were interested. It is not surprising. And you were, of course, checking once more on the little crow.

Didn't expect Jill to look up at me, did I? Clutching her letters there. Thought she'd just go on by. Hadn't occurred to me she might want to come up and see what I'm doing.

The loft is after all her property.

Get with the head shaking. Thought sends shivers down my spine.

Maybe you should smile too. You don't want to seem unfriendly.

I'm doing my best.

"You mean we're banished?" Jill isn't looking too pleased.

Why would she want to see anyway?

There is such a thing as natural curiosity, especially among family members.

I'm not really frigging family. How can I be?

She did indicate earlier that she would like to assume you are.

She can assume what she likes.

She is not going away. She is still looking up at you.

Yes, she is.

Say you indicate you are preparing a surprise—something that will be revealed later. For works of art such as this—murals—I believe there are often unveilings.

"You're not painting nudes up there, are you?"

The idea of it!

No, no, I'm not.

Wouldn't know a naked woman if you saw one.

"I suppose no nudes is something of a relief."

Relieved or not relieved, she is waiting.

I'm trying the unveiling thing but I don't really know how to do it. Anyway, I'm too bothered. I can't think straight. Why doesn't she go inside to check through those envelopes?

"One for you, kiddo."

Can't be. Not even if she is waving it at me.

"It's from Wendy. Must be the copy of that missive from your father's lawyer. She said she'd send it."

Why would she do that, when she's already said what's in it?

She may have thought you would want to see it.

Well I don't. Means I'll have to think about it again. I can do without that. I don't need another upchucking disaster.

Nevertheless.

I've put it out of my mind. I'm busy. I've almost forgotten about it. Trouble with the second tree is it's harder. If I hadn't remembered about that stuff in art class—

Perspective!

Quite the little genius.

Yeah, perspective. Like with the telephone poles we had to draw.

Trouble is I'm not sure I'm good enough at it. I figured out how I have to start the top of the second tree down lower to show it's a bit more distant. I don't know if it's going to work though. I don't know how I'm going to fit all the other trees in, now I'm getting to that.

My supposed letter's going back with the others.

"I'll leave it on the kitchen table. You can pick it up when you want to."

Jill's taking off, thank frig.

That top's kind of low-cut, isn't it? I was almost looking down on her… No, I don't need to be thinking about her boobs. What I need is to be getting back to work.

You may have missed your chance.

Shit, Scott's coming out now. He has his briefcase with him like he's going somewhere. He's looking my way too.

Definitely should've got out of here.

"You were up early."

Shrug on that one.

"Good of you to be so quiet. If we hadn't seen your plate in the sink we wouldn't have known you'd been there. You're not usually up ahead of us."

Not usually, but today. Slipped over to the kitchen while I was wrestling with the second tree outline. Thought some food might help.

Is Scott going to the car? He isn't. "I'd like to give you an update on the day's plans. Can you come down?"

Have to, won't I? Annoying Jill's more than enough for one morning.

You are so smart so often.

Nice to have Ingen taking his hat off and making his bow for me.

OK I've made it. I'm standing in front of Scott, as commanded. I'm giving Scott a salute. He likes that. He's clicking his heels together. He's saluting back at me. "Item one: we're going to the city for groceries. We thought you might like to come with us."

Good thing I've still got the paintbrush in my hand. Makes it easier to show the grocery store isn't high on my list right now.

"OK I know it isn't exactly the most appealing prospect in the world." Scott's giving me a wink. "Still we thought you might like to get off the property again."

I'm suggesting maybe some other time.

"We also need to make sure you'll be all right by yourself here since, as I foresaw, the need for that has now arisen. We have to visit our banker. He likes to get us both together."

Show at least a hint of reluctance. Just a little, not too much.

That I can manage. Jill's coming out again. She's carrying what's probably the grocery list. Also a shopping bag.

"Kyle's going to stay," Scott's telling her.

Doesn't like that either, does she? "He's hardly been off the place."

Guess she's still trying to figure out whether or not I'm "normal."

Up with the paintbrush.

"Well, I suppose it's OK. I know what renos are like once you get started."

Whew! Settled.

"But Scott, have you warned him?"

"I haven't had the chance yet."

Warned me of what?

Is the queen coming to visit? Am I going to have to give her a tour? Will there be cheering crowds? Police, security guards, bomb threats?

I do not see that as a possibility but I like your spirit in suggesting it.

Better get serious. Scott and Jill are.

It's Jill who's opening her mouth. "There's the crow. You've got to know she could go any time. I've put a blanket on the porch. If she does, all you need to do is cover the cage with it. We'll deal with the burial."

Kind of changes things, doesn't it? Bit like a punch in the gut. But she's all right now. She's alive still. I can see it. She's still sitting there.

Death is not ever predictable. It can take but a moment.

Jill's reaching out to touch me. AGAIN. "If you want to change your mind…."

Scott's agreeing. "If you think you can't face it…."

If the crow's dying, she should at least have somebody nearby, shouldn't she? If they're not going to be here, I have to. Which I'm showing.

Scott's giving me a look of approval. "You're a good lad."

"We'll be as quick as we can, I promise." Jill's approving too. "I've written my cell number by the phone. You can always call me."

Weird how she believes I'll do that. Considering speech would be necessary. Considering she has noticed I don't talk.

Still if there was some emergency, it'd be different. Of course, it would. I'm not going to stand by and let anything terrible happen to anyone. Not if I can avoid it.

This wouldn't be an emergency though, would it? Emergencies are something you can do something about.

Maeve's getting up. It's like she knows now she's on duty. She's leaning against my leg so I can feel her at my side.

There they go. Scott and Jill. In Scott's car together. I'm waving. I'm giving Maeve a pat and she's taking herself off. Not very far. Where she can still see me.

Always wanted to be alone here. Should be celebrating.

Can't with the crow though, can I? Doesn't even feel right going back to the loft again.

There is the paintbrush.

Yeah, I do have to deal with that.

Can't believe how many times I've been up and down to the loft today already. Once more does it. Got the paintbrush in the thinner jar.

Second tree truly is beginning to look like it should do.

Second tree is NOT what I'm supposed to be attending to. Yes, yes. I am going down and I am crossing the yard again to the porch. I am doing that ONE MORE TIME as well.

Little crow, little crow, little crow.

Little crow, can I interest you in this flower? It's yellow. It looks like the sort of thing crows might eat. Or play with even. Crows do play, don't they?

Little crow, please don't look so miserable. I don't even have to open the cage door to give it to you. I can push it through the wire. And nobody is going to hurt you. I promise, I promise.

You've got to start taking care of yourself. You can't go on like this. Above all, please, please, don't die.

Wonder if you're lonely? Wonder if you'd like some other birds about? Say I flap my arms. Say I do some pretend soaring, for you. Hop about where you can see me, sort of squatted down.

You are not very crow-like.

Don't even need my dad to tell me I'm acting kind of nutso.

Finally seen it for yourself then, have you?

But anything's worth a try.

Sitting's so depressing. Makes we want to poke at her. See if that'll work.

Wouldn't poke you, little crow, though, would I? Wouldn't, wouldn't, wouldn't.

Maybe I'll go in the kitchen. Had the last of the Coke for breakfast. What else is there? Iced tea, a whole great jug of it. Homemade and everything.

Should've expected it. Jill said yesterday iced tea's the only thing keeps her going when the weather gets hot. Which it is. Hotter than yesterday.

Weird how it feels so different now the house is empty. Now the two of them are gone. Hey, I could go into their office, have a better look round.

But the letter is on the table.

The letter is where Jill said it would be and I'm ignoring it.

I'm going to the office. Not that anyone's ever stopped me going there, of course. It's different on my own though. I can look MORE ACTIVELY.

Snooping, are we?

What if I am? Snooping's not so bad. Snooping's useful. You have to when you're always in different places. Only way to learn what's what.

As I recall, the good doctor—Doctor Who, he who helped you conjure me—snoops a large amount of the time. I myself am also a snooper.

Ah, ha! The phone. With the cell phone number by it.

Don't want to spend too long at this. Not into abandonment. Crow's had enough of that.

Hadn't noticed that funny little guy with the propeller hat on top of Jill's computer. Wonder where it came from?

Not too hard to see who's tidier. Not too hard to know it isn't her. View's nice, out over the garden. I can see where I was digging for the worms. Office books look boring. *River Deltas Analyzed. The Bulrush As Filter. Ponds: An Urban Case Study.* Ones in the living room are better. Hey, here's this one I've been meaning to read. The one on the ascent of Annapurna Scott says is great.

Hell, what am I thinking? I've got to stop frigging about. Back out through the kitchen then. Maybe I'll make myself a sandwich.

The letter is still on the table.

Maybe I won't.

If you are going to return outdoors you could take the letter with you.

What's up? Why are you bothering?

It is my job to look after your interests.

All right. All right. I have picked up the envelope. I have taken it in my hands. Good enough for you?

Quite something really. My very first FAMILY LETTER. Return address? Children's Aid Society. Sure does tell it like it is.

Might as well get my thumb under the flap. Might as well open the sucker, now I've got this far. Unfold the paper, typed so neatly

Get with that heading. *Bowles and Smythe, Solicitors.* Might as well go for broke. Take in the oh-so-personal greeting: "To Whom It May Concern."

Am I concerned? Yeah, I suppose I am. And, since I am, guess I might as well keep at it. Might as well keep reading to the bottom of the page.

Eighteen

"I AM WRITING ON BEHALF OF MY CLIENT, MR. HOWARD MCGINLEY."

That's my dad, all right.

Address says Bowles and Smythe are in Vancouver. Must have gone as far as he could get.

"Mr. McGinley has instructed me to be in contact with the Children's Aid Society regarding his son, Kyle, whom he believes to be within the Society's care."

How does he know I'm alive even? That's it though, isn't it? My dad just knows things. He has his methods. I've watched him with people. Seems like he can find out whatever he wants. He's nice about it too. They don't even notice. Mr. Smiley!

"Mr. McGinley is aware that for some time now he has been unable to fulfill his responsibilities towards Kyle in an appropriate manner."

Why is the page shaking? Why is it doing that?

"He has, however, been facing circumstances beyond his control."

Would it have taken so much to send a letter? A proper one. Even if you're in prison. Shit, he hasn't been in prison. He's too clever. I know that.

"He wishes to inform you—"

Could they cut all the crap?

"—to inform you that his regrets are sincere and that he would like to be in contact with his son once more."

Contact? He wants to see me? No one said anything about that. Guess Wendy was in too much of a hurry. Or Jill was too mad. Could there have been other letters like this? Could it be no one took any notice?

What does it matter?

If my dad wants to see me…

Your father is a man who has not exactly treated you kindly.

The letter said there were "circumstances."

Which you know full well cannot come close to justifying your father's behaviour.

Could Ingen shut the frig up?

But all I have seen would indicate—

Yes, yes, I know. Getting locked in the closet, the car rides. They did happen. I didn't make them up. But there's nothing I've ever wanted more than this. All these years, underneath it all really. Even though I know it's crazy. I wanted it right from the beginning almost when I went to the mailbox, after it was emptied even. Every shitting day.

I suspect there may be more direct cruelty than you have revealed to me.

The finger-jabbing that was supposed to be funny? The way he'd twist my arms? Suddenly, doesn't seem to be so important.

Perhaps you should give yourself some space to think about it all, reconsider the matter of the sandwich.

No, no, NO.

Take some air.

Maybe that though.

Yup, yup. I'm back by the crow again. Only thing I can remember I'm supposed to be doing. Sitting with her.

Little shithead.

I'm not little any longer. Maybe bigger would change things.

Maybe it wouldn't. It should also be noted that your esteemed parent does simply seem only to wish to make contact.

Contact's a beginning.

There is no mention of seeing.

Contact's a whole hell of a lot more than I've had so far.

Holy shit! Tears are coming out of my eyes. They're running down my cheeks. I don't even know for what.

Maybe they're for the crow. Still frigging sitting there, still frigging huddling. Doesn't have a mother either, does she? Maybe her mother died too. Maybe she's like me that way as well.

Wish I could remember mine. Can't though, can I? Wasn't even a photo of her. She's just some great frigging black hole. Everyone else at least has relatives. I don't. Not that I know of. Grandmas, grandpas. Sending presents at Christmas. Packages.

Come on. There's only one person I'm going to cry for. Only one I can really belong to. Like other kids belong to their...

MY FATHER. MY FATHER.

DAD, DAD, DAD.

Wish I could end this. Wish the tears didn't keep on coming. Feels like I'm going to cry forever. I'm going to wash myself away. Snot, gob. It's like all the crying I've made myself not do is pouring out of me. Leaking. Like at the beginning.

If you will turn your head, just a little, you will see something extraordinary.

I don't want to turn my head. I don't want to do anything but think about how my dad wants to see me. Contact me, at least.

Gently, my boy. I am not seeking merely to distract you.

Might as well look, mightn't I? After all, I know Ingen's not going to give up.

Snot, gob.

OK, OK, I'm turning my head. I'm looking.

Holy shit, it's the crow. She's looking back at me. She's stretched out a foot. She's sort of swaying. She's moving. She's coming towards me.

It's as if she wants to make me feel better.

Can't be. I've got Maeve's head in my lap. She came directly. Dogs do stuff for people though, don't they? Birds are different.

Perhaps there is something in her past. Crows are creatures of extraordinary intelligence.

Get real. This isn't some stupid movie. It's not Disney.

Does it matter? What more knowledge do we need? For some things, there is no explanation, only mystery.

At least the tears are stopping.

We have wanted her to move and she is moving. Can that not be enough?

Guess it can. Guess it has to be.

So what about me then?

I haven't forgotten you. It's just…if she's moving, maybe she isn't going to die. Maybe she'll start eating.

Could be it's just coincidence.

I do not think so.

Frig, she's got her head on one side. She's got sounds coming out of her.

She may wish for some response. Not everyone has a desire for silence

I don't talk crow.

"Crow" does not seem to be what she is speaking.

Weird. Sounds more like chicken. Pok-pok-pok-pok-pok. Cluck, cluck, cluck.

You recognize it?

Of course I recognize it. Chicken's something I practised. There was that ad on TV I got into imitating because I liked the way the chicken was standing in the middle of the screen. I'd do it when I thought no one was listening. Walking to school even. All by my lonesome.

I can't just start clucking though, can I? Isn't clucking speaking?

Little crow. Little crow, you're sinking down again. Little crow, little crow, don't give up. I'm here for you. Listen: "Pok-pok-pok-pok-pok."

Frig, she's liking it.

If she's liking it, I've got to keep going. "Pok-pok-pok-pok-pok."

Strange to hear my voice again.

"Pok-pok-pok-pok-pok."

She's liking it and she's looking interested. When she hasn't been. Not in anything.

Little crow, I'll cluck my heart out if that's what you're wanting. I'll pok from here to the ends of the earth.

Nineteen

SO NOW I HAVE A PET. FROM HEREON IN, THE CROW IS MINE. DON'T
know whether to be glad or sorry. Wish I didn't have to be doing
this to her. Putting my hands around her, lifting her out of the cage.
Seemed like a good idea when Scott and Jill suggested she might
do better with more freedom. Doesn't seem so good this minute.
Doesn't seem so good at all.

Easy. Easy.

I've got her against my chest. I'm holding her like I wanted to
when I first saw her. I was right though, wasn't I? She's terrified. Her
heart's going a mile a minute.

Shouldn't have been so eager. Shouldn't have agreed.

But Scott and Jill were so pleased. They came back. They saw
how she was. They'd been away longer than they'd expected. She
was eating and everything, clucking away there.

They said I'd worked a miracle. They said we were "bonding."
Should have been onto that one, shouldn't I? Dangerous adult word.
Bonding's what I'm always supposed to be doing.

The crow doesn't have to bond. Not if she doesn't feel like it.
I don't care about her bonding. I care about her flying. I thought
in the loft she could practise, when she's ready. And Scott was so
certain. Jim-cat'll get her if they let her go wandering about down
here.

Shit she's thin. There's nothing to her under her feathers. She hardly weighs anything either.

If you are going to take her....

I've got to start walking. I've got to get her across the yard.

Could just put her back.

Trouble is there's the pokking. I can't seem to get it out of myself when I think Scott and Jill can hear. Feel like I've got my own hands around my throat or something.

But that's selfish.

Only I can't seem to do anything about it. And the crow needs it. It's what keeps her going. I just went in for lunch. Time I came out she was all drooped again. That's when I made my mind up.

Not long, little crow. Not long.

We're almost in the barn bottom.

As we have seen, the unexpected is always a possibility. Once we get there....

Could be, couldn't it, Scott and Jill are right. Could be she does need her freedom. Lucky they left me to it. They've kept Maeve in even.

Going to have to do a bit of juggling. Can't hold the crow in both hands any longer. Need one for balance going up the steps.

What if she has a heart attack? What if I kill her? She's so warm though. Warm and soft. Kind of want to nuzzle her under my chin.

Can't do that. Can't do anything but keep on going.

Weird she's so still. Weird she isn't struggling.

Not unusual, I think, for birds in such situations.

Glad to hear that.

Animal farm, is it?

Never had a pet before. Don't know if I even thought I wanted one.

Shall I try a bit of chicken now? Actually better if she doesn't start moving. Don't want to drop her.

Right, I'm up. Wonder where should I put her? Under my trees maybe? Would she like it there?

Might drips of paint present a problem when you are working?
Guess they might.

Let's go for a corner then. I can bring hay. I can make a nest for her. It'll be somewhere for her to come back to.

Slowly, slowly.

There. There, she's down. Still not certain, is she? Worse than that. She's not even looking around. She's into the cowering.

Give her a minute.

But it's not what's supposed to be happening. It isn't at all. Maybe if I get back into the clucking: "Pok-pok-pok-pok. Pok-pok-pok-pok."

All right when I'm on my own. When I'm on my own I can do it. I can do it, but she's not listening any longer. It's like she's gone away. She's in some place where she can't hear me.

What do I know about crows? I don't know anything. Ingen! Ingen, help me out. How am I going to get her back? Make her hear me?

Try one more time.

"Pok-pok-pok-pok. Pok-pok-pok-pok."

Really couldn't do this if I was in the yard, now could I? Everyone'd be at me. They'd say, if you can talk to the crow, why can't you talk to people? They wouldn't be able to see it's different. They'd get some frigging psychologist. Maybe that's why I couldn't when I was down there. I just knew, didn't I? Even without thinking about it.

Whatever. Seems like I have to hurry. I have to do something. I don't think waiting is going to be good for her. I have to do something now.

It occurs to me that there are, in fact, cases of prisoners who miss their cells.

You've got to be kidding.

I am not. The cases are well documented.

Are you trying to tell me she could be missing her cage?

Perhaps it is home to her.

So why didn't you say so?

I also am afflicted by a weakness for believing live things should have their freedom.

If it's the cage, I can get it. I'll go now.

Better start remembering about the floor flap. One I had to push up when I first came here. One that covers the hole at the top of the steps. Haven't been bothering with it. Better start though. Big thing is I've got to keep her safe.

I am sprinting. I am crossing the yard again.

"Everything OK?" Jill. She's calling out the kitchen window. Must've been watching. Probably couldn't help herself. Don't want to stop. Just want to keep on hurrying. Point at the cage then. Pick it up.

"You're sure you're going to need that?"

I'm sure. I'm nodding.

"Your call. You're the wonder-guy."

Not exactly how I'm feeling. Don't have time to argue though, do I?

"Do you need a hand?"

I don't. I can manage. Not that getting the cage up is easy. Frigging thing's so awkward. Bits of wire sticking out all over. Almost falling to bits.

Done it though, haven't I? Up with the floor flap. Down again. Crow's where she was. Feel like I betrayed her.

This is not the moment to be worrying about that.

She can't really want to be in this contraption, can she?

That is not for us to be deciding.

Guess it isn't. But she isn't perking up at the sight of the thing. She's still not moving.

She's too frightened.

Should I lift her in?

I think you are going to have to.

One more time then. Frig, frig, frig. There you go, little crow. You're back again. Really do hope that's what you're wanting. What about the door?

In my estimation she will need you to shut it.
I'll be shutting her in though.
Probably we should know that changes need to be gradual.
She is looking kind of happier.
She will perhaps not require any of this forever.
I give in. The door is closed.

Holy shit, wouldn't have believed it, but it's like she's sighing in relief. I can see her spreading herself almost. Ingen, Ingen! You are a GENIUS.

Here I go then. "Pok-pok-pok-pok. Pok-pok-pok-pok."

She's into it. She's got her eye on that piece of carrot. She's eyeing it. And she's picking it up.

"Pok-pok-pok-pok. Pok-pok-pok-pok."

She's looking at me like she's pleased with herself. Down the carrot's going.

Yes, oh, yes.

She's opening her mouth again. She's pokking back. Means there's a chance.

Disaster averted.

Little crow, I'm a pokking machine. I am at your service. Especially if you're going to drink your water. "Pok-pok-pok-pok. Pooooook-pok-pok-pok." I am the famous chicken-speaking human, the one you have been looking for. I might even be able to rescue you. Give you back your life.

"Pok-pok-pok-pok. Pooooook-pok-pok-pok."

"Pok-pok-pok-pok. Pooooook-pok-pok-pok."

Shit, can't seem to help it. I'm looking at my trees.

Thing is little crow, I have other work to do. How are we going to deal with that?

I won't desert you. Of course, I won't. But I started something. I liked doing it. I want to get on with it.

"Pok-pok-pok-pok. Pooooook-pok-pok-pok."

As you are demonstrating pokking can be quite loud.

What's that got to do with it?

It means I would consider painting and pokking a distinct possibility. Perhaps, as long as the crow is able to hear you, she will not have need of your actual presence—not close up.

Hadn't thought of that. Could kind of move away as an experiment. Doesn't seem to be minding, does she? She's into the bird chow. When it comes to eating, probably needs to be catching up.

If I could just do a bit.

"Pooook-pok-pok-pok. Pooook-pok-pok-pok"

Wonder where I should start?

Getting to seem more and more as if I'm going to have to give that first tree a second coat. Probably means I'll have to do that for them all. Like the way the paint's soaked into the wood. Makes it more natural.

"Pooook-pok-pok-pok. Pooook-pok-pok-pok"

Should I at least try getting the brush ready?

I myself would definitely attempt it.

Out of the paint thinner. Wiped on the cloth. I could open the paint can up.

Looks like the crow needs a rest anyway. She's sort of easing into herself.

Paint needs a stir.

Good boy. Gotta tell ya, I'm looking forward to seeing this.

That's my dad's voice! Can't be. Not saying that.

Didn't want to get in the way before. Glad to be on the scene again.

My dad who said maybe he wanted to see me.

Who I would remind you is also a figment when it comes to being in your head.

Where the frig did I put the letter? Guess I shoved it in my pocket. Does say it, doesn't it? My dad is sorry. He has his regrets. It does, it does really.

There's this part as well I never got to. Too busy crying. There's a second page. That says there'll be "a further communication." It says my dad just has to "clarify his plans."

Plans for what? Is he coming? My father, MY FATHER. If he's coming it'd be good to have something to show him.

Why would I want to look, little shithead?

Not complete redemption?

How the hell am I going to work out what I'm supposed to feel about all this?

At the moment there is no need.

But I'll have to sometime.

Sometime, maybe. For now, you can concentrate on other priorities? You can get yourself back up the painting ladder.

Guess I might as well. If I don't you'll start nagging again, won't you, Oh Lord of Ingenuity.

Think I'll leave the first tree for the moment. Paint probably needs to settle more anyway. Yeah, yeah, I'll start on second tree fill in. Pokking all the while, of course. Shape needs something more though, doesn't it? Like…like a hole in the middle that could have been made by some animal. A hole I'll need to leave bare.

Better begin with the outline for that.

Really do seem to have got the perspective right. Don't think it was much more than luck though.

Before I do much more I should probably make myself some kind of diagram. I should work out how many trees there are going to be in total, figure out properly where they're all going to go.

Twenty

IN MY OPINION, TIME FOR A BREAK

Guess it could be.

"Pok-pok-pok-pok. Pok-pok-pok-pok."

How long have I been at it? Thing is now my arms are stronger. My legs don't hurt so much when I'm going up and down the ladder. I can keep on and on.

Perhaps not always an advantage?

But the trees are always calling to me. Look at them. Glad I stopped at five. Five is awesome. It's great. That one tree in the middle, those others, two on each side. Not in a line either. Dotted about. The way I wanted them. The way they are in the swamp.

Each one's different too. They're different but they look like they belong together.

Couldn't have managed without those sketches I made on the floor. Can't believe it took me two whole days and then some, figuring them out. Worth every minute. Especially once I realized the trees at the back weren't just going to have to be smaller, they needed to be vaguer. Vaguer means a lighter touch.

Ten days the whole thing's taken. Checked today on the calendar in the kitchen.

You have come down the ladder. You are on the ground even.

One, two…and three! Three trees with two coats done. Two's perfect. Trunks look all sort of rough still. If I put on more paint, they'd be too smooth. It's the second coat on the other two trees I have to get to. That and the water, of course. STILL have no clue about that.

You began working at dawn again.

Never thought I'd be a dawn person, did I? Almost getting used to it. Don't have much option considering it's when Lady C gets into clucking, greeting the day. Really goes at it.

Lady C. Lady C.

When did I start calling her that exactly? Can't EXACTLY remember.

You are starting to climb again.

Just seems to suit her. Way she holds her head up. Way she's got so shiny. Bigger, prouder.

Still wish she'd come out of her cage.

You have opened her door many times.

Yeah, and she's shut it. Couldn't believe it the first time. How she hopped over. How she stretched out with her beak. Pulled it tight. No mistaking what she was up to. I'm still leaving the catch off.

You are starting on another branch.

I stopped to get food! I took Scott up on his offer of "polishing off" yesterday's lasagna for lunch, didn't I? I didn't even hurry. I listened to him and Jill talking about that earthquake that's happened, how they're going to send money. I waited till Jill had finished going on about her difficult client.

"A real asshole, if you'll pardon the expression!"

I even grinned at her to show I didn't think the pardoning business was required.

All that is further in the past than you imagine.

How much further?

Quite some hours. We are well into the afternoon. You have said yourself also it is sometimes better to go away for a while.

Maybe it isn't better right now.

"Pok-pok-pok-pok. Pok-pok-pok-pok."

Talking to Lady C is no excuse for refusing some relief to yourself.

I know. I know. She doesn't actually need it any longer. But she does like it. Gets her excited. Makes her hop up and down. Entertaining herself though mostly. Pulling those hay stalks in through the wire. Looks like she's weaving a pattern.

Means I have something to tell Scott and Jill. They like their little updates. Jill especially.

Of course she wants to come up here. See for herself. Bit of a pain, always putting her off. Not that it's that much trouble. She and Scott do seem to get it I'm doing something that matters to me. They seem to like it I'm excited. ENTHUSIASTIC.

I am craving the sunshine.

Actually think now I should stop myself. Just got to come down, tidy things up as usual. Don't want the paintbrush getting all hard. Don't want the paint getting that skin on.

Need a minute to give Lady C a tickle though.

Like your tickles, don't you? There, on your chest through your feathers. Puts you in a trance almost. Can't get enough of it. Tongue thing doesn't seem to be bothering you, does it? Wings are growing too, I think.

"POOOOOOOOOK-POK-POK-POK. POOOOOOOO OOOOOK-POK-POK-POK."

You are becoming excessive.

How do you know? Might be I've laid an egg.

For heaven's sake.

Don't get snarly. I'm going to give you a spin on the tractor.

Who'd have thought, friend Ingen, I could learn so quickly? Who'd have thought Scott would put the key on a hook in the barn here so I can use it ANY TIME I WANT?

Here I am then. Down the ladder. In the seat again.

Got to rev the engine. Scott told me to do that in case there are creepy-crawlies in the exhaust. Not too bad at reversing now, am I? Gate's a pain, of course. Down, up, down before I can go anywhere. Can't exactly drive right through it though, can I?

Love this moment when I first hit the field and the open. When the sun blasts on me, and the wind.

You will notice that the grass is not as green as it was when you got here.

You can say that again. Scott and Jill are talking about the dryness all the time now. They're calling it a drought.

Wave for old Daisy cow. Scott does that always. Not that she seems to notice.

Doesn't matter the tractor's so frigging ancient. Still makes me feel like I'm king of the world. Especially when I'm going faster. When I've got it in high range. Nice knowing my way around. Having it familiar.

Hey, there's that bird Scott told me about, the one that's called a killdeer. Does the broken wing thing. Recognized it, didn't I? How about that?

Got to admit it. Kind of miss having Scott with me. Standing at the back there. It was sort of like…

Having a father?

Guess so.

I truly am sorry I've been so bad about that.

Goes for me double.

I really do believe maybe now I could do better.

You could? You reckon?

Must I continually caution you.

Little shithead.

Still confused, aren't I? Hits me at the weirdest moments. Never know when they're coming. Noticed though mostly my dad's a lot quieter. He's just not saying so much. Sometimes even says good things about the painting—way I'm doing it.

A fair time has passed. A time when the promised "communication" does not appear to have manifested itself.

Like all the other promises? Fishing trips we were supposed to go on. Bike I was supposed to be getting.

Thought you deserved it, did you?

You see? You see?

Yes, I do. Makes me feel like an idiot. Like a little kid always trying to get some candy. Can't seem to stop though.

How about giving the good old tractor a bit more throttle? Scott was funny about that. He said doing it reminded him of his grandfather and how he was always calling him a "young punk" for wanting more speed.

Pedal's a nightmare. Scott was right. Hand gadget's better. Nice hearing about his granddad. Wonder if I'll ever meet his mom? She phoned once. Scott seemed to like talking to her.

No one's ever phoned for Jill. Not family, that is. People phone for meetings. Lots of them. They come here too. It's the wetlands thing. Jill's always wanting to introduce me. I'm always bugging out.

Jill's the one I've got to watch for. She wants me to be going places, spending my allowance.

Wonder what the hell she thought was going to happen when she informed me she'd found out not-speaking is a condition? It's called elective frigging mutism. Did she really think it'd get me gabbing, bursting into song? Take more than that. Helluva lot more. CAS kids are always getting labels on them. Too this, too that. I'm used to it.

Wonder why she had to call Wendy to tell her what my condition is? And then tell me she'd done it. Wendy knows I've got my own pad even. Jill said she felt she had to tell her about that too. Guess I should be grateful. Seems Wendy suggested they should "let matters lie."

Big thing I wonder is what it'd it be like not having some agency getting consulted about me all the time. Got to be better. Could be frigging marvellous.

Does it cross your mind ever you might wish to stay here?

Would if I let it. Won't do that though. Do think I could get used to it. Even with Jill being so sparky. Day she found out Lady C's clucking probably meant she'd been raised with chickens was really something. She was all set to find "the perpetrator." Took

Scott to remind her there's apparently more than one chicken keeper round here.

*If you are going to keep allowing your thoughts to churn, you
would be better to go back to your painting. Why are you not looking
at the scenery, relishing it?*

Yeah, why not? Loving it, all of it. How the tractor's throaty roar
is throbbing right through me. How I can go around the field as
many times as I want to. Stop, start, wherever. How I have my hands
on the steering wheel. Making all the right turns. Getting myself
onto the track that leads off to the woods.

Wish it didn't go past the pit. Does though, doesn't it? Frigging
car I wrecked is almost covered with daisies. White ones, nodding
their little heads to themselves.

But still you notice it.

Yeah, I do. I do but I'm not going to let noticing stop me going
where I frigging want.

Have to turn around now I'm at the woods, of course. Track's too
narrow to take the tractor under the trees. Sometimes I make a tight little circle, doing the brake thing. Today I'm going for a big swinging arc.

Haven't been under the trees in a long time. Haven't been to
the stream. Too busy. Did see last night how the moon's growing.
Thought how soon I'll be able to go back to my rambles in the dark.
Looking forward to that.

OK, OK, so we're back by the car. I haven't forgotten what I did.
Doesn't make me afraid now though, does it? Have this feeling maybe I didn't need to be so scared in the beginning.

My thoughts exactly.

I am who I thought I was. I'm not going to find myself suddenly
doing something like it again.

Rumble, rumble, rumble. Rumble and roar.

Be where I can see the house soon. Movie night tonight. Some special
DVD we're going to watch. Jill says it's funny. Quite like going over there
now, don't I? Just don't want to live there. Move back. GO TO MY ROOM.

And here we have the cattle. Cattle again. Always round the water trough now, aren't they? Scott has to keep checking it. Making sure it's full.

Wonder what's for supper? I'm hungry. I think, too, Jill said something about how she wanted me to water the garden. Got to keep being the good boy. Don't want my "privileges rescinded." What social worker threatened me with that one? Maybe it wasn't a social worker. Maybe it was a teacher. Can't even remember what the privileges were.

Nice that Scott's come out to meet me. Nice to have him opening the gate for me, guiding me into the barn. By myself I'm always a bit afraid I'll clip the fender on that old washing machine, or else go charging through the wall.

"You're doing brilliantly. Truly a star pupil!"

I do like it when he tells me I'm good at this.

Another new experience?

Kind of!

How about a high five to show him I've been enjoying myself? How about a bit of pretend Harley-ing, so he'll know I remember he gets off on that?

Wouldn't it be something? Having a dirt bike? Having it here?

He's clapping me on the shoulder. Don't mind him touching me. Guy thing. Still not so certain about Jill.

Shit, is that a vacuum cleaner I can hear whining its heart out? A vacuum cleaner in the house? Daily sound at Mr. and Mrs. Household Products. Not so usual here. Is something up?

Scott can tell I noticed. Looks like he's about to enlighten me. Maybe why he came out here. Maybe it wasn't just for the pleasure of my company after all. "I thought I'd warn you developments are developing."

Developments? Adult word for shit breaking loose.

"The fact is Wendy's coming—tomorrow, first thing. She called us. We thought we should clean up a bit. We don't want her to believe you're living in a pigsty. Anyway, we want her to be comfortable."

Great day ruined. All in an instant.

Have to brace myself. Get ready. Only thing I can be certain of—she won't be coming for anything good.

Don't be so sure, son. Remember the further communication. Ten days isn't really so long. I had matters I had to attend to.

Oh my god, could it be there's been another letter? Could it? Could it?

I'm doing what I have to. I'm putting one foot in front of the other, walking beside Scott towards that vacuum cleaner sound. I am. I am. We're at the porch almost.

But my head is spinning. Spinning, spinning, spinning. Round and round and round.

Twenty-one

"WE MIGHT AS WELL GET DOWN TO BUSINESS."

What we're here for. All of us together in the kitchen. Brand new morning. All of us looking at one another, wondering what's going to happen next.

Except Wendy, of course. Wendy's pulling her chair out. Wendy's not wondering. Wendy's in charge.

Shit, wish Jill hadn't decided I wanted scrambled eggs for breakfast. She's got weird all of a sudden. Kind of smother-y.

She is concerned for you.

Every two minutes last night, through the movie, she kept looking at me. She kept asking if I was all right. Don't know if I was or I wasn't. Don't know now. Do know I didn't sleep much.

Thinking about your dear old daddy?

Yeah, I was. I was thinking about my dad. I was thinking about finishing my picture. I was thinking about Lady C, how I want to see her fly.

I'd hoped you might be filled with excitement.

I was sometimes. Only sometimes I wasn't. There was dread too, wasn't there?

I would say so.

Let's get to it. Let's sit down.

Around the table. Like when I first got here. Jolly little gang.

"So, Kyle, I hear you've been painting."

What's painting got do with anything?

Wendy is simply trying to be friendly.

I don't see why.

"You have a pet, too. That's the first time, isn't it? I gather it's a bird. You've been a part of a rescue operation."

I get it. Something else for the frigging records. Pets must mean I'm making PROGRESS.

Couldn't we just get on with it? Couldn't Wendy tell me—

She is opening her briefcase.

"I was so sorry about what happened before. I really did want to talk to you all in person this time."

In person don't mean nothin'! I just want to see what she's bringing out.

It would appear to be…

Oh, my god, it is. It's another letter. She's putting it on the table. I can see the heading: *Bowles and Smythe.*

My dad.

"The lawyer again?" Jill should keep out of it.

This might, of course, affect her also.

Nothing like as much as me.

Say I reach out. Say I just grab the paper, read it. Why do I have to wait for the "announcement?"

"It's hard to know where to begin. It's all so unexpected." How come Wendy can look and I can't? "I won't go into the details."

Probably thinks I'm too stupid to understand them.

"The fact is what this letter represents is a formal notification that Kyle's father is going to apply for the termination of Kyle's wardship."

My wardship? My wardship? He wants me out of the CAS?

Told you I'd be in touch again, didn't I?

But I couldn't even imagine. Not really. Not last night even. When I was sort of hoping even.

MY DAD. MY DAD WANTS ME.

That is not what the letter says.

Must be what it means though. Why are Scott and Jill frowning at each other? Why don't they like it?

If you father's application is successful, you will leave them.

There are plenty of other foster kids. They can always get someone else.

Perhaps they do not want someone else.

What difference will it make to them?

Holy frig! Jill's wiping her eyes. She's got tears in them.

Scott's getting something out of his wallet.

I believe it is a photo.

A photo of what?

I imagine it to be a photo of his brother.

The brother? The dead one? Hell, I'd forgotten about him. Hasn't exactly come up in conversation, now has he?

Why am I bothering anyway? This isn't about them. It's about me.

It's just...I don't know. The photo. The way Scott's fingering it, fiddling with the edges. I can't help looking. I can't help wondering what he's thinking.

I don't need his shit though, do I?

"It would appear the previous letter was then simply a means of laying the groundwork."

You might have known you could trust Scott to keep calm.

Wendy's looking like that's a relief to her. "It's what we think at the CAS. I've talked to my superior about it."

Jill's leaning forward. Jill's really not pleased. "Can he succeed in this? I mean, given his record."

Don't any of them get it? That my dad might want me.

I suppose I will after all have to admit it is a possibility.

Don't any of them see what it would mean?

Time to be together again.

Time to be a normal person.

Wendy's pushing her hair back. She's sighing. "Under other circumstances, I would say it would be extremely difficult."

They'd try to stop him? They don't know him. They don't know my dad can do anything he wants.

Even abandon...

Frigging doorstep.

"What's different now then?" Jill's voice has an edge to it. "Scott and I have to know this."

Isn't the person who has to know this me? Apparently not! It's Jill who's going to get the answer.

"What's different is that Kyle's coming up for his sixteenth birthday. That means his wardship is automatically up for review."

Up for review? That's the first I've heard of it.

Jill's face is thunderous. "Has Kyle been told about that?"

All eyes on me.

I'm shrugging. No, no, no. I FRIGGING HAVEN'T.

"Shouldn't someone have warned him?" Hell, Jill's icy. She could freeze your balls off.

Wendy's sitting up straighter, preparing herself for the attack. "Yes, Jill, they should have. If they haven't I apologize. I haven't been his social worker for long. I assume no one mentioned it because it didn't occur to us his father would appear on the scene."

Hardly surprising, really.

But they told me. They kept saying the CAS was with me forever. Till I'm eighteen.

"We believed the review would be a formality. We didn't foresee there might be any challenge."

"Surely—surely..."

"I'm afraid, Jill, there is no 'surely.' I'm afraid courts are funny things. They're not always predictable."

"You're trying to tell us the courts could agree to this?" Scott's still holding the photo.

Everything's back to Wendy. "I'm afraid I am. There are precedents in fact, and once a ward is past sixteen there are no half measures."

"No sort of guardianship? No follow-up?" Better be careful. Jill might explode.

"I'm afraid not."

So I could be on my own? I wouldn't be a package any longer? Why does that suddenly seem so scary?

Because it would be.

With my father?

Scott's coming in again. "Jill and I are in this for the long haul. We're only just getting to know Kyle. We think we have quite a lot to offer him."

"A helluva sight more than—" Holy moly, Jill's so mad she's speechless. Scott's put the photo down. He's got one hand over hers now.

Nothing like family, is there, son?

No, no, there isn't.

All those other places just don't cut the mustard.

"There is something unofficial that's going to come into play here." Shit, Wendy's actually turning towards me. "It's called the sneaker law."

"And what might that mean?" Why doesn't Jill butt out? I don't want her running interference.

"The sneaker law means, Kyle, that ultimately where you go is up to you. The courts know you're of an age. You can vote with your feet. You can't be made to stay anywhere you don't want to. Even if your wardship is terminated, you're going to be able to choose what you do about it."

"So it's all right. We could keep him? He could stay with us?" Jill's sitting back. She's acting like everything's settled. Didn't she hear? It's if I want to. Shouldn't she ask me?

"He could on his own authority."

Surely they're not expecting me to make up my mind right now.

"He wouldn't have to leave school even. You would get no further support money but he himself could apply for Student Aid."

"We don't need the money. I told you."

"Jill's right. The money's not an issue."

The issue is ME. MY FATHER. We're all that matters.

I would not agree with that exactly.

"It's kind of a lot for us to get our heads around." Good old Scott.

Wendy's relaxing. "I know that and I'm sorry."

The letter's going back where it came from. I never even got to take a look.

"Clearly too we have some leeway. Notice has not been formally served and Kyle's birthday is two months away."

Might be the birthday of all birthdays.

Meeting's almost over. I know the signs.

"Still, I wanted you all to have as much warning as possible."

Did Wendy really say I'd be the one to do the choosing?

"Now, Kyle, this painting." Frig, she's changing the subject. "I'd love to see what you've been up to."

"He's told us it's a surprise. He hasn't shown us even, has he Scott?" Jill's in there, like a shot.

"Indeed he hasn't." Scott's giving me a wink.

I can't wink back at him. I don't want to. He can see it too. I can tell by the way he's putting the photo back in his wallet. Sort of sadly.

Wish he'd let me see it. No. No, maybe I don't.

Anyway, we're back in the nicey-nice stuff. Wendy is being gracious.

"I guess then I'll have to return one more time. In the meanwhile I cleared my schedule so I could at least visit your garden."

Scott's getting up. "Of course, of course. We'll take you."

Jill's attempting a smile. "Kyle can show you where he's been watering."

He can, can he? I'm not a three-year-old. Doesn't occur to her, does it? Waving the hose about isn't exactly at the top of my head right now.

Looks like I'm going to have to tag along though. Looks like it'll be easiest. At least they won't be able to talk about me when I'm there.

Twenty-two

WENDY SURE IS LOVING THE GARDEN TOUR. "THOSE TOMATOES are wonderful. And look at those zucchini."

"We'd be happy to give you some." Scott's bringing a bag out. He's filling it up.

Is that it? Are we done? Seems like it. We're heading towards the driveway. Wendy's into last-minute messages. "I'll let you know if anything else materializes.

"Don't hesitate to call me.

"Kyle, I truly am sorry to spring this on you, especially when it seems you're doing so nicely here, although we are worried—all of us—that you're not talking. I'm not too sure about this barn thing either."

OK, lady. I'm worrying about myself now. Not for the same reasons, of course.

At least the visit's over. Wendy's opening the car door. Wendy's getting in. She's starting up, departing. Her arm's coming out the window waving.

"The man's an asshole." Shit, shit, shit! Jill's back into it. "You know what I believe?"

Of course I don't. I don't even know who she's talking about. Not for certain.

"I think your father's playing with you."

We're going into the kitchen, but that's not what I want. I want to be by myself. I want to be in the loft again. It's like she's got me cornered. Like I've got no space.

"Jill—Jill, wait."

"No, Scott, I'm not waiting. All these years and all of a sudden—"

What does she know?

"I bet he doesn't want you now any more than he did when he left you."

Come on, Scott, stop her. She's scary. She's plugging the kettle in but it's like she's wrestling with it. I'm backing up along the counter.

"We're talking my whole childhood."

HER childhood. Where did that come from? What about mine? Isn't Scott's dead frigging brother enough? Who else is in this?

"That was it, wasn't it? My father! My beloved daddy. Pushing me away from him, dragging me back."

"Jill, I think we should—"

"Well, I don't."

Scott, Scott, please. Get your butt over from beside the window. Do something. Don't just flap your mouth.

"I think Kyle has to know about this. He has to know he can't get his hopes up."

Whose hopes are they? We haven't even got to sit down. We're all standing about here.

"My father was always doing the exact same thing. Reeling me in, then abandoning me. He left me with aunts. I'd just get settled. And I was such a sucker. I was in university even. He made it sound so tempting."

It's not THE SAME. It isn't.

"He'd make all these promises."

My dad hasn't made even one.

"I'd be sloughed off. I'd be dumped again. Know what he did? Know what he did the last time? He left me on a street corner with no money, no way to get anywhere."

"I think Jill's doing her best to let you know we want you."

Right, buddy, you're out of it, aren't you? You're no help.

Jill seems to be making herself a cup of coffee but the water's spilling. "Of course, we want you. That's not all there is though. What I'm really trying to tell you is that you shouldn't be touching your father's overtures with a ten-foot pole."

Wendy said… she said I could do my own choosing.

So why am I suddenly in some contest? Why does it suddenly feel like what really matters is whether or not Jill can win.

Yell at the bitch!

Trying to get between us.

I hate arguments. I hate them.

Uppity little snot-face.

Fix her! Fix her!

Clear out of this. I'm not you, Dad.

GO ON! GO ON!

No, no, I won't.

She's asking for it.

She can ask all she wants, I'm not giving it to her. I'm not giving it to anyone. It's not my way.

"You have to understand. You can't just let him…"

Someone's got to put an end to this though, haven't they?

"It's all about him really. It's never, ever, ever going to be about you."

How does she know? She can't. She doesn't. Why does she think I'm such an idiot? Why does she think I need her frigging advice? It's her dad she's on about. HER DAD.

"You let him do this now he'll be doing it forever."

There's a knife on the counter. I can see it.

Didn't get the lawyer letter, did I? Waited when I didn't have to. Didn't get the lawyer letter. But I can get this.

Only takes two steps. There it is. The knife. It's in my hand. I have it.

Worked too. Jill's not saying anything. Scott isn't either.

IT'S MY FRIGGING TURN.

I've got the knife. Inside me it's quiet.

I'm holding my thumb up. I'm running the knife blade along it.

Yeah, yeah it hurts. It hurts me. No one else though. The blood's coming, just like I wanted. Not much, but enough.

I'm going to the fridge. The blood's for writing. Red on shiny whiteness.

The blood's for giving MY message.

F.O. F.O. F.O.

Twenty-three

HOW MANY DAYS HAS IT BEEN NOW?

Three. I personally have been counting.

Three and nothing's happened. Got to hurry though, haven't I? Paint, paint, paint, paint. Do know waving knives about is pretty much a cinch for getting you kicked out.

Surprised Scott and Jill even let me get through the door. Surprised they just stood there, watching me go. I'd put the knife down even. They could've stopped me.

Paint, paint, paint, paint.

Even more surprised they didn't call the cops. Could have. Might have happened. Where would I be then?

Bet there's a million, trillion other phone calls winging around out there. Discussing my "outburst." So much for Wendy's "doing nicely." Who knows where I'll get put next? Have to do something with me till the wardship thing, won't they?

Be some group home most likely. Managed to avoid that so far. Except for those first few days, of course. Won't be avoiding it any more.

Picture's the big thing. I've got to get it finished before I go.

Trees, trees, trees.

I so relish the way you are putting your heart into them.

Don't know why they seem so important. Just know they do. Partly it's for themselves. Partly it's for having some good memory to take with me. First time ever. Sure as hell isn't so Scott and Jill can look at them. Touching little memento after I'm gone. They're so cagey, the two of them. Just let me waltz back in when I was hungry. Don't know how I managed that myself quite. Just know I did.

Jill even said something about how it was her fault. She's sorry. She keeps on about it. Almost every time she sees me. Don't get it.

Probably all part of the CAS-type plot. Keeping me STEADY, till someone somewhere's worked something out that's "appropriate." Someone somewhere who isn't me!

Two whole months to my birthday. Two to "under review." Two to when…shit, my own choosing!

What am I going to do with it? It's not what I'm used to. One thing I do know. I don't want to go and live on the streets. I've seen those kids. I don't want to be like them. Turns my stomach, even thinking about it.

I'd kind of like to finish school too, even though I hate it.

Really do wonder why my dad's gone so quiet. Can't even remember last thing he said.

Wonder too why Scott and Jill haven't taken the F.O. off the fridge? Holy frig, I could've got moved just for the F word, just for the F letter. Let alone…

Brandishing a weapon?

Brandishing a weapon. Right.

Paint, paint, paint, paint, paint.

Do know it could happen any minute. Why I have to keep at this. Why I can't stop. Whole thing's looking so good too. All of the trees filled in now. Two coats wherever needed. Just those few branches. Stark, stark, stark.

Haven't been back to the swamp again, what with one thing and another. Not enough moon yet anyway. Still truly does feel like I've got this right.

Don't know why I thought I should add these little bushes on the left here. Kind of fiddly. Seems like I need them though.

Bushes mean taking longer but the whole thing has to be as perfect as I can get it, even if I have to stay at it night and day.

As you are doing.

Yes, I am.

Problem's still the water. Maybe if I put on a whole lot of coats I can at least get the shine to it.

Shit, it's hot. Good thing I've got my shirt off. Was tempted to go for my jeans as well. They're sort of part of me now though. They've got so much paint on them. Almost as much as the wall.

Pok-pok-pok-pok-pok.

Yes, Lady C, I hear you.

How about I open your door just one more time?

Still the same old same old? Still wanting it shut, are you? Don't you get it? There's more to life than cage-wire weaving? Done a pretty good job of it though, haven't you? Only got the top part empty now. Made your own artwork. Worked in those ribbons I found in the basement when I was looking for the smaller brush.

Oh, so what you really want is a tickle. Here we go then, with a "pok-pok-pok-pok-pok."

You'll be all right, you know. Scott and Jill will look after you. Scott and Jill are actually good people.

Although you seem to have no regrets.

Couldn't see any other way, could I? Knew I had to stand up for myself, make my point. Knew too, right from the beginning, this place is too good to last.

You may note I made no comments during the episode.

Yeah, actually, I did.

I believed you could find your own way. I was certain you could manage it.

Thanks for that, buddy. Yeah, yeah. Thanks.

Thing on my thumb was nothing. Not much more than a scratch. Hardly even needed the band-aid Jill made me put on it. Bet the CAS'll get me with that one too though. Bet they'll say I'm into that "cutting" stuff people keep talking about.

When bodily wounds are self-inflicted?

Is there nothing you don't know about?

Here's something else that's weird—way Scott and Jill have started going on about school. How it won't be long before I'll have to register. How they have to get in touch with the local high school. Why would they bother, when I won't be here?

Must be another part of the good old keep-him-steady plot, I guess. Not exactly necessary. Wasn't planning on doing anything un-steady. Wasn't planning it at all.

Being in the house is horrible. Scott and Jill are so frigging careful what they say to me. Like they're taking each word and having a look at it before they let it out. Never wanted that. Never wanted Scott to stop joking.

Guess it's only what you'd expect when there's a criminal living with you. A violent offender.

Paint, paint, paint, paint.

Wouldn't even go for meals if I didn't have to. Meals, shits and showers. Can't stay longer. Can't bear it. Can't think about Scott's brother. Can't think about Jill's daddy.

Paint, paint, paint.

OK, so the bushes on the left are finished. Wonder if I'm going to need some on the other side?

Balance is, I believe, important.

Got to stand back and take a look. Reckon I'm going to have to go for it.

At least I can do the bushes from the floor. Don't have to get up the ladder.

Frigging hot there, at the top. As it is, every time I move I start sweating. I've been sitting in a puddle, my own personally created sea.

Good thing I brought that other paint can up. Reckon I'm going to need it. When I get to the water especially. More than one extra can, in fact.

My dad may be quiet but I can't stop thinking about him.

Hoping?

I don't know. Trouble is I keep feeling he's going to appear out of the blue. Be like him. I keep going to the window every time I hear a car. Which happens more often than I need. Gather the wetlands project is getting urgent. People aren't just having meetings. They're getting together to make signs. To put on their lawns, I guess. Jill says they're strategizing. She keeps trying to fill me in on it.

Imagine what she'd be like if I hadn't done the knife-thing. She'd be wanting me to help. At least she's given up on convincing me I need to meet the neighbours.

Tempted to wave at them sometimes. Don't mostly. Doesn't seem much point. There are all these guys I don't know though. Makes me realize I'm not really sure what my father looks like any longer. Makes me wonder if I'd recognize him.

Guess that's why I almost went searching for him on the Net. Yesterday, when I thought I could keep it a secret. When Scott and Jill were out. Went into their office even. Sat myself down at Scott's computer. Got to Google. Far as it went. Didn't even key his name it. Couldn't bring myself to do it.

"Pok-pok-pok-pok." Come on, Lady C, come out of there. Do it, just for me. After all, I'm not going to be around to see you flying, am I? Least you can do is let me see you strut about.

No, no. I'm not interested in seeing you poop. Even if you are going to do it anyway. I've seen enough of that. It's why I've got the newspaper under your cage, now isn't it? So I can keep you nice and tidy. So I just have to pull the paper out. What's left of it. The bits you haven't managed to tear up.

To be used for decorative purposes?

That'd be it.

"Pooooooook-pok-pok-pok. Poooooooooooook-pok-pok-pok," Yes, yes, yes. You're dancing. You're so clever. Not as clever as me though. Look at those bushes. Aren't they the best? Only need one coat for them, although they did take some thinking time. Trouble with the water is I'm going to have to let each coat dry before I can do the next.

Could take days. Really, really, really should've started sooner. But I couldn't. I hadn't worked out the shiny thing at all.

Going to have to stop now too. Hand's so sweaty. Can't hardly even hold the brush. Also, if I don't get myself a drink I'll die. I'll turn into a leaf, all dry and withered. Someone'll find me, lying here gasping, opening and shutting my mouth like a landed fish.

How can it be so hot? What the hell's happening?

I would say there is high humidity.

Air feels like it weighs a ton.

Almost 100 percent I would imagine.

You really are the scientist, aren't you, Ingen?

Indeed, I am. I am in agreement with you about the heat too. As you may notice even I have had to remove my lab coat.

Not down to your skivvies though, are you?

Certainly not!

Big question is whether I should go to the tap in the yard or head into the kitchen for a Coke.

Once more into the breach perhaps?

Coke's what I'm wanting. Can't make anything any worse now, can I? So, Coke is what I'm going to get.

Twenty-four

ALMOST THERE. ALMOST GOT MYSELF ACROSS THE DESERT WASTE. Well, actually the yard! Air feels worse now if you can believe it. Thicker. Like you could cut it off in blocks.

"We can't wait, can we? We've got to tell him."

"Of course we have to. We've got to tell him now."

Holy frig. Words are floating out the window. Scott and Jill are talking. Guess what too? They're talking about me. Giving me the chance to get some advance info.

Say I just stand here quietly, over to the side a bit. Holding my breath.

Not exactly hard to guess what they've "got to tell me," is it? Sounds like I'll be loading my duffle bag into some social worker's car tomorrow. Probably even Wendy's—if she's still around, of course.

I have so often warned you before against jumping to conclusions.

I should go back. Get on with the water. One coat'd be better than nothing. One coat at least.

Can't tear myself away just yet though. Need to get the details. Yup, here from the side'll do it. DO NOT want to get caught. DO NOT want phantom skulk-er added to my crimes.

Bet they're sitting down. Bet they've got themselves some coffee. So they can discuss the rest of my life.

OK then. Who's next?

"We're going to have to tell him and I'm going to have to shut up. I can do it now, I promise. It's why I kept what he put on the fridge— so I'd remember. Not that I'll forget. I won't forget ever. How could I have been such an idiot?"

Jill's into the "it's my fault" shit again. Means I'm going to get more of the "so sorry" from her. Only this time it's going to be "so sorry you have to leave."

Bet it'll be a relief to them, getting back to their cozy little life.

I don't know how you can say that. I don't really.

Why shouldn't I?

"I think it has to be today." Scott's going on.

"Of course it does. It's not right, keeping things from him, especially if it's about his father."

My father?

I did warn you about jumping to conclusions.

"Oh, Scott, I can't believe the man's coming here."

He's coming? My father? He is?

Reason you haven't heard from me. I've been busy. I've been making my travel arrangements.

"Be simpler if we knew when he's arriving, Jill-O."

"Or if he's really going to. I can't help it. I still have my doubts."

In which she may be justified!

Not now, Ingen, I don't need you getting in there. Not now. Not now.

"Wendy said he was on the road somewhere. He was calling from a phone booth in Calgary." Scott's adding this bit.

"Presumably so no one could trace him."

"He's still going to have to get our address from the CAS. Kyle has to give his say-so for that."

"He'll give it, Scott. Of course, he'll give it."

Holy shit, Jill's crying again. Properly this time. Is she crying for me?

"Do you think he knows we really want him?" Her voice is so wobbly.

"I can't answer. I can't tell. Maybe I shouldn't have been so insistent about giving him space, letting him do what he wanted. Maybe he thought it meant we couldn't be bothered."

No, I frigging didn't.

"Maybe he took it the wrong way."

"But there was Tom, your brother."

In the photo.

"You were so sure you knew what Kyle would need."

"Maybe I was wrong about that. Maybe I should have listened to you more."

"Do you think he cares about us at all?"

"I don't know about that either."

"It's so not what we planned, Scott."

You might care if you would let yourself.

"Having him not speaking, living out in the barn there. It's why I came to the end of it—partly. I'm not patient the way you are."

Jill has actually shown patience beyond believing.

More than anyone else has ever.

"Oh, Scott, Scott—there've been so many times I've wanted to give him a good shake."

"I've got to say I didn't imagine him grabbing a knife. I never thought of that."

"I pushed him. I pushed him and pushed him. I'm the last person who should've done that. I should've known. Why do you think I went back to *my* dad all those times? I had enough people telling me not to. I always had to give it one more go."

She understands?

What she's been saying about sorry. She meant it?

"The knife was a shock. I think I was even more stunned by what he did with it. I thought he was going to attack. I was getting ready. Man of the house stuff!"

"But Scott, Scott—all he did was hurt himself."

Bet I know what's happening. Bet Scott's got his arm around her. Bet he's comforting her. Wish I could see it. Can't move though, can I?

Sounds like Jill's still crying. Way she's blowing her nose.

"Perfect parents. That's what we wanted to be for him, wasn't it?"

Another blow. Louder.

"It was ridiculous, my friend. Perfect's not possible."

"If he'd just believe me that I'm sorry."

I do now. I get it.

"But we're human. There's his history. We can't take all the blame."

Little shitface.

"The big thing is I have this feeling, at heart, he's such a good kid. He's just kind of quirky."

"Quirky's up our alley, Jill-o."

"We got it all mixed up with our own baggage and now his father's coming. Kyle thinks I'm against him but I love it he has his own stuff he wants to be doing. It may drive me crazy but I actually love it he wanted his own place. I have so much admiration for him."

Admiration? No one's ever said anything like that about me. Don't think they ever thought it.

"He's our kind of guy, Jill. I'd hoped we could take him climbing."

Climbing!

"What he does with his hands when he's telling us things. It's so ingenious."

Frig, there are more tears coming. Now Jill's blowing her nose AGAIN.

You could just go in there.

No, no, I can't.

Why not? What is stopping you?

It's making everything harder. All of it. ALL OF IT.

But those were good things to be hearing.

That's the problem.

"One thing we could do, Scott."

"Bring it on, kid."

"We could tell him the door's always open. Even if he goes, he can come back if he wants to."

"I'd be up for that. I'd be up for it with bells on."

"We'll do it next time he comes over."

Next time. Next time.

Hell, it's getting darker. It's raining, pouring, great big drops.

Could it be, my boy, that you have found people who could love you?

It could. It could but there's nothing I can do about it. Not right now. I'm going back to the barn. I'm getting under cover. I'm going up my ladder, my stairs.

To hell with the Coke. I don't need it. I don't need anything. Except maybe to be where there's something I'm making. Something that came from out of me. Something I'll always have.

It's all right, Lady C. Here I am again.

Don't look too frightened, do you? Don't look as if you're bothered one little bit the rain's pounding on the roof.

Getting louder too. LOUDER AND LOUDER.

There are all these crashes.

Lightning's coming.

God it's scary. No, no it's exciting. Coming and going, filling the room.

The power of it. The strength.

The everything. All the storm thing.

Makes me want to dance. Leap, spring.

No, no. Makes me want to get painting.

Not the trees. The trees are for calmness. This is something else.

Twenty-five

WHAT THE HELL HAVE I DONE?

You have painted the tumult. You have put it on the wall here.

Have I? Really?

Guess I have.

Storm's gone. It's moved off. Except it hasn't. It's alive still. Alive there on the wall. Like it's the most alive thing you could have.

Kind of want to sit down. Kind of feel...I don't know. Maybe a word I've never used before.

Awed. Yes, awed.

Still wet outside, still raining. Only gently. A patter, with a rhythm to it. On the ground below me. On the roof that's over my head.

I've never been so frigging stunned in all my life.

It is your creation and it is a delight to me.

Thanks, Ingen. Thanks for that.

POK-POK-POK-POK. POK-POK-POK-POK.

What's that, Lady C? Are you raising a cheer?

You're not? You're more interested in having a drink of water? It's OK, I can take that. You're a crow. You have your needs.

Didn't think when I was doing it, did I? Didn't think. Not once. Just let it happen, come out of me. That great big circle with all the lines from the edges, the middle of it. Those thick, wide splotches whacked right on.

Must have jumped, I guess, getting to those high bits. Paint couldn't have landed there by itself.

Do remember running. Sprinting across the room. And yes, there was leaping. The louder the storm got, the brighter, the more it went on and on.

And still it is not chaos.

It isn't. There's a shape to it, an order. It's like nothing I ever imagined.

It is vibrant, magnificent.

I never imagined it. I couldn't. Only now it's like something I've always wanted to be doing. More than the trees even. Only there's some way they're not really separate. Trees, storm. They go together.

Of course, they are both yours.

I suppose they are. Couldn't have one without the other. Wouldn't have known how.

Kind of a mess on the floor.

Holy shit, I'm paint all over. I'm going to have to shave my hair to get it out.

No, no I'm not going that far.

Good thing Lady C's cage was out of the way or she'd have got splattered. Shit, what if I'd hurt her?

Didn't though, did I? You're fine aren't you, My Lady? Tickle, tickle, tickle. "Pok-pok-pok-pok-pok." You are just so, so fine.

Lots of puddles outside. Huge, great big ones.

Hey, there's Scott and Jill. They're coming out. They're grinning at one another like all the wetness is the best thing ever happened.

Which, given the dryness, it is.

Not everyone'd notice that though, would they? Not everyone'd be thinking about it. Sure as hell wouldn't be catching raindrops on their tongues, the way Jill is.

They really, really are people I like.

People who like you. You should not forget that.

Except I don't know how to believe it.

I am certain you can manage it, if you give yourself some time.
But I've hurt them. Jill especially.
You could do something about that. It might not even be that difficult.
Even if it is, I should at least give it a try. I should, shouldn't I?
I owe it to them. I frigging WANT TO. As much as I've wanted to
do anything for anyone. Ever. Ever, ever, EVER. That I can remember anyway.
Not going in again, are they?
No, they're not.
Just standing there, enjoying each other's company. Grinning
away at it all.
Should get to it, shouldn't I? Get my sorry ass on down there.
Before I chicken out.
Wish me luck, Lady C. Give me a pok to go out on.
POOOOOOOOOOOOOK, POK, POK, POK.
POOOOOOOOOOOOOK, POK, POK, POK.
Hey, the full on I've-just-laid-an-egg thing? Thank you, My Lady.
Thanks for that.
Don't you worry. I'm going to be careful. I'll close the floor flap.
I can't have anything happening to you. I've got to keep you safe.
First step out into the yard's a bit tricky, specially because they're
looking my way. They can see me already. They're staring at me.
"What in the world?" Never entered my head Jill'd start laughing.
Didn't cross my tiny mind she'd do that. Makes me want to laugh
back. Wiggle my hips a bit, start grooving. "What the hell have you
been doing? You look like leopard man."
Leopard man? There's an idea then. How about I get my arms
going, liking I'm stalking. How about I show my FANGS.
"You are the biggest freak I've ever come across."
Sounds like a compliment. Scott's getting in on it. He's shaking
his head at me. "Pity they don't have those freak shows in the circus
any longer. We could've made money off you. We could've charged
people for a look."

"I suppose we could turn him into an artwork. Put him in a gallery."

Calls for flexing my muscles. Nice bit of posing.

"I think memorialization's the name of the game here." What's Scott on about?

I would say he means he wants to take your photo.

"For sure, Scott. We need this for the scrapbook."

Nod, nod, nod, nod. Give them a shrug or two. OK with me.

"I shall return, carrying said camera." Scott's heading in. There's just Jill and me. We're alone together. We're looking at one another.

Can't help it. I'm hanging my head.

"Could we call a truce, do you think?" she's asking me.

I'm trying to tell her I want to go beyond that. I'm nodding as hard as I can.

I think she is, as you would say, "getting it."

I hope so. I'd like that.

Scott's coming back. He's setting up a tripod. "The light's not great. It'll take a flash, I think. Where would you like to stand, my lad?"

Stand? Where would I?

Only place that seems right is the middle of a puddle. Got to splash about first though, get muddy. Add to the effect.

"That is all very well but this is not video. Ultimately you are going to have to hold still."

All right. I can do it. Still as a rock. A tree.

Once and once for luck. Show's over.

"Want to see what you look like?"

Laughing at myself now. Can't help that either. Picture's OK, But I'd like something of the three of us. Maybe they'd give me a copy. Let me take it with me.

Not too hard to show them how I'm hoping it might be.

Jill's kind of blushing. "I could go for that," she's saying. Her face has gone all lit.

"Brilliant. We can send it to all our friends for Christmas. How about it, Jill-o?"

"It'd have to have a title."

"Shouldn't be too difficult. 'Drowned Rats' seems pretty obvious."

"Where are you going to put the camera?"

"Depends if we're going to be in the puddle or not. If it's the puddle I can leave it where it is."

"Puddle seems perfect." Jill's wading in. Scott's getting everything set up. He's got the timer gadget going.

Quick sprint. He's with us. We're together. All three of us. In the water, up to our ankles.

It's me that's in the middle.

"Better do the luck thing again."

Scott. Jill. I'm putting my arms round both of them. Camera's flashing one more time.

Rain's stopping. Too bad Maeve isn't here. She should've been in it. Don't think I'll worry too much about that. Scott and Jill are what matter. They're what's important.

Hell, all of a sudden, I'm freezing. My teeth are starting to chatter. I'm wrapping my arms around myself.

"Scott, my friend, we've got to get this man inside. He needs warming up. He needs a blankie."

"Maybe a hot toddy?"

"A bath'd be better."

"We should also get him into some dry clothes."

They're taking over. Don't have much option except to go along. Do I want one? Don't really. Happy enough to have them bring me in.

Into the kitchen, where Maeve is, wagging her tail at me as ever. Maeve and good old Jim-cat, licking his good old crotch.

"You take him upstairs, Scott. You get the water ready. You're the guy."

"I'll get the clothes too."

"Remember this, Kyle. After the bath, there will be supper. We've got steaks, prepped and ready."

"Red meat to set your pulses racing, and put strength in your kneecaps."

A bath, dry clothes, steak? Might even be baked potatoes. Sounds like heaven. Steak and baked potatoes. I can handle that.

Twenty-six

"GOOD NIGHT, KYLE!"

Good night to you, Scott.

"Good night! Sleep well. It's been some day."

Good night, Jill. I'm off across the yard again. Avoiding what's left of the puddles.

Thinking and thinking how "some day's" right.

Some day. Some evening. Bath was amazing, nearly scalded my skin off. Couldn't get the paint off, of course, though they did give me some thinner to try with.

Paint had got too settled. Guess I'm stuck with it a while.

Moment when I got out of the water and it seemed like Scott had forgotten about bringing me anything else to put on was scary. He'd taken my jeans away, for shit's sake. They were in the dryer.

Thought I was going to have to go downstairs stark naked. What an idiot. Didn't occur to me I could have wrapped a towel around me. Clutched my hands to my good old private parts at least.

Should've known better. Should've trusted.

There I am, standing there dripping. There's Scott's hand round the door.

Couldn't believe what he brought me. T-shirt with that stupid balloon face character he's got on his cooking apron. One he made so much fuss about my first day. Doesn't have a cupcake on it. There's this guy with black hair looking all miserable lying on a couch. Balloon is saying, "Helium."

Scott says I can keep it. It'll be "his pleasure."

Apparently it's from some cartoon on the Net. He says he'll show me. Didn't tonight though.

Surprise, surprise. He's a jockey man. Don't know how he can bear it, going round always with his balls so tight. Didn't tell him I'm into boxers. Didn't seem right.

Shorts he lent me are ridiculous. Beach things. Palm trees waving.

Rather fetching, actually.

Not what I'd have said.

Frigging freezing right now. Sure is colder, out here in the yard. Got to get into that sleeping bag, pull up the hood thing, hunker down.

Steaks were awesome. Potatoes had sour cream with them even. Sometime when we were eating Jill managed to get it out about my dad. Scott said how I could come back whenever I wanted. Think I look surprised all right. Don't think they suspected I already knew.

After supper, there was a slide show. Scott said it offered comic relief. Amazing. There were shots of Jill dressed up like a belly dancer. They were so not like her. There she was though. Couldn't mistake her. Veil and all.

We were in the living room. It was cozy almost,

Cozy is not a word I have heard you use before.

Doesn't feel like I had the chance.

Almost tempted to go up to my room, sleep inside for a change. Scott and Jill would've liked that. I might have even. Only there's Lady C. She's never been on her own through the night before, not since I took her up here. Where I'm going. Up the ladder to MY PAD.

So there we are, Lady C, I'm coming. I'm lifting the floor flap. I'm pulling on the light switch.

No, NO. SHE CAN'T BE GONE.

It can't have happened.

But it has. She's not in her cage any longer. The door's open. I should've kept using the latch thing.

Did Jim get up here? He couldn't have. He was in all evening. He was sitting on my lap.

Also he is not Super-Cat. The floor flap was closed. I cannot really see him lifting it.

So what else has been here? If I find it, I'll frigging crush it. I'll smash it to bits.

You might try looking on the window ledge.

The window ledge? The window ledge? What the hell's she doing there?

I think she has found it is the time when she can come to her freedom.

Couldn't she have waited—so I could see her?

Her time is what I said.

Yeah, yeah. You told me. You said that, didn't you, how it would be.

But, Lady C, you got me so frightened. It was like this humungous kick in the gut. Still getting over it. Can't believe it. Clever of you, though. Really clever. Looks like you've been asleep. Had your head under your wing maybe. Way you're blinking.

Hope I'm not now scaring you. Don't want you going back. It'd be the worst. I'd hate it. Don't want you in that cage at all. Unless it's where you want to be, of course. Unless you like your coming and going.

Look around. I would say she has been having quite the time here in your absence.

Frigging hell, my boxers. She's scattered them all over. What are you, Lady C? Some kind of pervert? Did you think they were going to attack you? Death of crow by shorts!

Would it be OK if I came nearer? I'd go carefully.

Doesn't matter? You're coming to see me? You're opening your wings, so you can hop down on them. Get your balance.

You must've used them to get up there. Next thing you know you'll be…

No, no. I'm not going to jinx this. I'm just going to watch you walking. Way you've got your head up. Way you put your feet down one at a time.

Still want your tickles, do you? Say I sit on the floor with you. You want to get on my lap? Let's move back so I can lean against the wall. So I can stretch my legs out.

Like it, don't you? You're settling yourself down.

Feet on my skin feel funny, scratchy. Your feathers are so soft though.

How's about that? We can see ourselves in the mirror. Weren't even here when I brought that up, were you? Didn't even know about you then.

Shit, I really do look kind of a mess. Paint splodge on my nose isn't exactly an improvement.

Mirror seemed important in the beginning. Then it didn't. Mirror's got paint on it. Everything has. That's the storm painting. Before that I'd been so careful.

You're out, Lady C. And you did it BY YOURSELF.

Hey, I should go tell Scott and Jill. It's what they're wanting for you.

Don't want to disturb you though, do I? Just want to have you where you are.

Anyway, they're asleep most likely. If I go over and start clumping about, they'll think there's an invader from Planet Zendron. Or some frigging idiot doing B and Es.

Remember when I brought you here? Remember how I held you? How you were frightened. Now look at us. Might even say this is cozy as well.

Say my dad was here. Say he's really coming.

That's right, buddy! Don't you go forgetting me.

If he was here, how would it be?

Probably think the storm picture's crazy. Probably want to get me locked away.

Might not, I guess. There was this place we went once. On a Saturday. We were outside. There were all these photos of insects to look at.

"Get a load of this, kid," he kept saying.

He asked me what I thought. He seemed like he wanted to know. For some reason, he was happy. He did leave me in a bar afterwards, watching TV while he was drinking with his buddies. But he looked at the insects with me. Praying mantis and stick things. Weird great beetles.

Wish I knew how long it's going to take for him to get here. If he's coming.

How the frig far away is Calgary anyway? How long will it take to drive? Guess it depends how often he stops. What he gets doing. Guess maybe I should look at a map.

You know what, Lady C? The other walls—the ones with nothing on them. They look so bare all of a sudden.

Say I put you up there? Would you like it? You're black. You're the colour of the paint I've got. Wouldn't mind having a crack at your portrait. Wouldn't mind that at all.

Twenty-seven

ALMOST LUNCH TIME. FUN TAKING THE TRACTOR OUT FOR A SPIN this morning. Good coming back here, have a stretch out in my bed place. Always good to do that.

Had to get out too. Driving me crazy, stuff that's happening. How long's it been now? Lost count AGAIN. Just know my dad is in Winnipeg. Or so he said when he called the CAS last night.

"Two and a half days away, if he pushes it," Scott says.

Wonder what he's playing at? Seems to have taken to using a cell phone. No way of tracing that either, I guess.

Almost got to admire him. Way he's tying up the CAS.

Wendy's calling every day—her boss even. They keep saying they haven't given out any information. They won't without my say so.

They still seem to think my dad knows where I am.

Fact is, so do I. Getting his own way's the thing he's best at. Rules and regulations are nothing to him. Wendy can crap on about restraining orders, whatever the frig they are. She can talk about the police even. Won't make any difference. He'll do what he frigging wants.

The CAS are not the only ones who are being "tied up" as you say.

No, they aren't. It's Scott and Jill as well. Wish they weren't. Wish they didn't have to be in on it all. Specially when they're so busy.

Jill says the wetlands timeline's growing tighter. There are all these meetings in people's houses. "Rallying the troops." They can't even go together.

"Over my dead body," Jill said, when I tried to tell them it was OK still, leaving me on my own.

Couldn't even argue. I don't know how I'd handle it if my dad came and I was all by myself.

Big thing I have to do is get in on these conference calls with them. At the computer, some program called Skype. Means we can all see each other. There's Wendy's face, and her boss's, staring out at me. Scott and Jill and me are staring back at them.

Shitting amazing how all of a sudden it seems so important TO KEEP ME INFORMED. Not exactly what I'm used to. More like, "we've decided," and "Here's where you're going."

Wasn't expecting Scott and Jill to ask me yesterday if my dad might be violent.

Not that that is quite how they put it.

No, it wasn't. Jill really is doing her best to hold back. I heard her tell Scott her tongue might start bleeding if this goes on much longer. That's how much she's biting it.

Not stupid though, am I? Do know what the words "pose a threat" might mean.

Pose a threat? I'm your father. Why would I even need to do that?

How the frig should I know?

Feels like I don't know anything about anything any longer. Specially when it comes to you. Thought you were out of my life forever. You were. Now you're back again. What the hell does it mean?

Oh, oh. Here she comes. Lady C advancing. Does love to get up here, doesn't she? On my chest. Way she starts the day. Still wish it didn't have to be so early. It is better when she goes straight for it though. Worst is waking up and finding her weaving hay strands in my hair. Makes me look loonier than ever. Can't seem to get the bits out.

Been busy with the mirror, have we, My Lady? Preening away at your feathers? Quite the Beauty Queen. Caught any spiders, this morning? Spider catcher extraordinaire, you are, aren't you? Must be pretty tasty, way you're gobbling them down.

No, I don't want you trying to undo my zipper. You leave my jeans alone. Bored are you? Why don't you go back to practising your flying? You're up to five steps on the ladder, remember. Why don't you go see if you can make it to six? Practising's good for you. Builds your strength up. All that opening your wings out so you can set right on your feet.

Wish I was going to get to see you do it. Out in the world there. Wish, wish, WISH I was.

Flying is, of course, featured strongly in your portrait.

How could it not be? It's what she's made for. That's why I did her so big. So I could have her stretch her wings out, reach from wall to wall. Glad I remembered to put in those feathery end bits. Like fingers.

There she is then. Just got to turn my head. She's coming in for a landing. Swooping, diving. Heading downwards after a long soar. She's been up in the sky for ages. She's been way, way high. She's loving it. The feel of it. She's got her beak open. I made it open so she could caw.

Here's the scoop, Lady C. It's what I'm telling you. You don't have to sound like a chicken all your life. Pokking's been good for you but you're a crow. You need crow talk.

Which she will come to in her own time, I am certain.

I hope, I hope, I HOPE.

Right now, I've got to get to finishing the water. Can't believe all the coats it's taken, in between all of everything else I was doing. Finally to the point where one more coat'll do it. Really does seem like it has the moonlight on it somehow. Like I found the answer, solved the problem, did what needed to be done.

Twenty-eight

HERE WE ARE. THIS IS IT. LAST NIGHT BEFORE MY DAD COMES. ONE more time to open the floor flap, close it. Look around me, see what I've done while I've been here.

Tomorrow'll be the day.

Trust my dad. This time, he got some other idiot passing on the info. Said it'd be the morning. From Toronto. Didn't say when, of course. Wouldn't go as far as that.

Got the call at supper. Scott took it. Came direct too. No going through the frigging CAS this time.

It's like I always knew. He'd find me. Probably why I didn't bother making up my mind about whether the CAS should give him my address or not.

Even Scott and Jill weren't surprised he'd got what he needed. Like they were expecting it as well.

"There you go, lad. It's up to you now," Scott said to me.

I just shrugged and nodded. What else was I supposed to do?

"Are you sure you don't want us to alert the CAS?" Jill asked me.

I knew it's what she wanted. She'd already told me. I've got to do this by myself though. I can't have anyone else mungling in.

"No back-up? You're absolutely certain?" Scott said.

Nodded even harder.

Scott and Jill gave each other a glance. Jill looked worried. I bet they're thinking about the violence. Wasn't easy for them, agreeing. I could see that.

Did though, didn't they?

MY OWN CHOICE.

Big thing I'm worrying about is how there's still the wall by the window that's got no picture on it. Been thinking and thinking about it. Seems like it's staring at me all the time.

Wall's so bare. Has to have something that's been important to me. Thought of the tractor. Thought of the cows in the rain even. Nothing seems to fit.

I would say there is only one thing you can put up there.

You would, would you?

I would say this last wall should contain an image of the artist.

You mean me?

Of course I mean you. Who else is there? The process is called "doing a self-portrait." It is a very common practice.

Seems a bit much.

You have plenty of time. The whole night is available to you.

People's not what I'm good at.

For heaven's sake, boy. Have I taught you nothing? Is not this whole room filled with risk and dare?

Guess it is. Guess I could at least try it. Start with a sketch on the floor, maybe?

I would advise you simply to go at it.

Here goes nothing then. Why the shitting frig not?

Get the paint ready at least. Take the brush up. Feel it in my hand. Know it so well. The weight of it. Got to admit it's lost a few bristles. Plenty left though.

Thing is, where to start?

Hair would be fun! Wild with all the hay stalks in it. Haven't had it cut all summer. Curlier than ever. Thicker.

Wonder if I'll need the ladder?

Life size?

Maybe a bit bigger. Should be able to reach though. Taller is better. Fills up more space. Maybe I'm going to grow too. Blankness above me shouldn't matter. I'm not the flyer. I don't go up there in the blue. Which would be black, of course, if I covered it. Black's where it's all comes from. Should've made the place gloomy. Hasn't.

Gloomy has nothing to do with it.

Nothing at all.

Isn't a whole hell of a lot of paint left. Don't want it to look half finished. Don't want to find myself running out of supplies.

Say I make the rest of myself cartoony. Just all lines.

Wonder why I put myself by the window, instead of in the middle? I'm not looking out, of course. I'm looking at my space. Which I claimed. I held onto. I MADE.

Could be I should frigging get on with it. Put the head in. Under the hair.

Do the body. Skinny. Skinny suits me.

After that it's all angles. Sharp a bit. Pointy. Shoulders, elbows, knees. Hey, I'm almost touching the window. Like I'm going to start leaning on it. Ready for whatever.

Like I'm some dude.

Other hand's got to go on my hip then.

And the legs? They've got to be crossed.

What about you, Ingen? Would you like to be in this?

I should like it greatly.

There's lots of room on the right there. Might be a bit faded, given the paint situation.

Faded is appropriate.

What d'you mean?

I am about to go, my work is over. It is time for my next assignation.

But you can't.

I warned you at the start I would stay only as long as I was needed.

My dad's going to get here.

He is and you, my boy, will find a way to deal with it. You have changed, grown.

You're my figment.

Figments come and figments go. They last in the memory, of course.

I don't think that's enough.

I am afraid it will have to do. Just watch what you yourself are doing. You see, already, you have put me at a little distance. I am away off in the corner.

That's got nothing to do with it.

Ah, but it has. I would ask you to be careful with my hat and lab coat. They are important to me.

Of course, I'll be careful. You're going to have to be cartoony as well though.

Cartoony and quite small.

I don't get it. Didn't you tell me, if I wanted you to go I'd have to send you?

Maybe I did and maybe I did not. For all and whatever, the adventure is over and it has been a good one. Together we have found a much-needed measure of success. Much needed and well-earned, I would say.

How come you didn't give me any warning?

Even the wondrous Doctor Who has only so many episodes.

Frig, Doctor Who. It's the Lord of Ingenuity I care about.

I am glad to have been of service. All paintings are actions of the mind and heart, you know.

What's that supposed to do for me?

Simply something to ponder. You should sign your work now. At least put your initials somewhere.

Like by where I am?

If that is your wish.

Are you insisting?

Yes, indeed. I would also suggest that you make them large enough to be actually visible.

Will that do it?

Most satisfactory.

Have to say it looks pretty good. Done too. Room is finished. Weird how the paint turned out to be exactly the right amount.

Guess I better clear up. Put the lid on the can so Lady C won't go getting in the dregs and stuff. Won't need the brush any more. Doesn't seem I should let it stiffen though. Better to stick it in the thinner like I've always done.

I believe before we part we might sit together. It looks to me as if Lady C is hoping you might provide her with a lap.

Is sitting all?

I must admit I am very partial to singing. I have experienced many farewells. If at all possible, I like a farewell song.

Don't think the Sex Pistols have any.

Rather fortunate. The Sex Pistols are to your taste, not mine.

The Sex Pistols were a joke. I was just trying to be funny.

Know something? I don't remember my dad singing ever. Scott and Jill do sometimes. They go at it together.

Sounds ridiculous.

There's his voice again.

You may note his voice is fading also.

It's because I'm going to see him. Larger than life. In all his glory. For better or worse.

Perhaps we might leave that lie. Perhaps we might get to the song. Do you know any shanties—sea ones? I am after all setting out on a journey.

Funny you should say that. Shanty's the only thing I ever did sing for anyone else to hear. I was in this choir. I was ten, I think. I don't remember the school or anything. I just remember I was stunned I got picked.

I had to stand right in the middle. Front row and everything. There were parents watching. I had this white shirt and black pants, like all the other boys did. Whoever I was living with came. I can see the mother's face even. Now I can.

She said I'd done great. She said she could see I was enjoying it.

And the song was?

Hold on, I've got to let it come to me.

If it is a sea shanty, it must be sung lustily.

You mean out loud?

You did pok for Lady C.

Meaning I can "haul away the anchor" for my figment?

You always said you would speak when you wanted to, although I do recognize that perhaps you will not be able to go full volume, not just yet.

More like a mumble?

Mumble on. Go with it. I might even join you.

Got the tune all right. Words are sad though.

Partings do have that aspect to them.

Think there's about four verses.

I shall expect to hear all of them. Goodbye, my boy. Good luck.

Twenty-nine

GOOD LUCK'S ONE THING. SLEEP'S ANOTHER.

Why the hell didn't I go for *Ninety-nine Bottles of Beer on the Wall*, or nine hundred and ninety-nine?

Anything but *It's Time To Go Now*. OVER AND OVER AND OVER. ROUND AND ROUND AND ROUND. What was Ingen thinking of, letting me get into that? Leaving me alone here.

Shitting earworm.

Where the frig is Ingen anyway? Having himself a holiday, on some balmy beach? Can't quite see it. Most likely really has gone on to his "next assignation," like he said he was going to. Sort of thing he'd do.

Kind of surprised me, when I got into it. Sound of my own voice. Guess hearing myself pok-king just wasn't the same. Thing is I was making words. Shaping them on my tongue and stuff. Don't think I was too big on the lusty. Too choked up.

One minute Ingen was there with me. Then he wasn't.

His bit of whatever it was we were doing stopped.

Hardly surprising Lady C's deserted me. Gone to sleep on top of her cage. Not exactly peaceful here, is it? TOSS, TOSS, TOSS, TOSS, TOSS. Will she need a goodbye song? I wonder. *I Want to Hold Your Hand* in chicken? Guess it could be a laugh.

And where the frig is my dad now? Could be close. Down the road in some motel, sleeping in the car even. Might be farther, in some fancy place.

Those frigging car rides he took me on in the night. Really were something.

Wonder where I'll be tomorrow? In a hotel too, with my father. Won't be home with him. Unless he's up and moved.

Say I really don't recognize him.

Say he doesn't show up!

Man for the big ideas, he is. All worked out in detail. Things we were going to do. Go on holiday even. Last minute there'd always be some reason why it wasn't happening. My fault, OF COURSE.

So, he's come this far but he really could turn round and go back. Leave his precious son on the doorstep again.

Don't know why I keep hoping. Can't seem to help myself. Just how it is.

Pretty good having his voice gone mostly. Sure don't miss that in my skull. Gives me more chance to think, for one thing.

If he does come, what'll he say to me? What'll I say back? Am I going to stick with not talking? Wonder how he might deal with that? Not sure what I'll do yet.

Probably should pack my bag first thing, be ready. In case of whatever.

Feels great having myself on the wall there. Me and Ingen. Had to have Ingen there as well.

Shitting hell, I've had it with *Time To Go Now*. I'm getting up. I'm taking myself over to the window, looking out.

Wish there was a moon. I'd be out of here. I'd go to the swamp. Weird how I never went back, not ever. Not once I'd started the trees. Couldn't seem to get myself to do it. Even when it was bright enough to see.

Hell, there's a light in the kitchen. I'm not the only one who can't sleep, I guess.

Wonder if it's Scott or Jill? Could be both. Could be there's been another phone call. Probably should go over and find out. Nothing to stop me. Lady C won't miss me. I'll just pull that cord, put the light on for when I come back.

How the frig often have I crossed this yard? Weird to think of not doing it any longer. Having it all end.

Should've known it'd be Jill.

I can see her through the window. Sitting there, at the kitchen table, in this gigantic T-shirt. Shit, she's looking sad.

She's coming to the door. She's heard me. Should have been quieter. Or maybe I shouldn't. "You too, eh?" she's asking.

I'm into the usual nods.

"Hardly surprising really. It'll be a big day for all of us. Want to come in and sit a while?"

More nods. Yes, I do.

Here I am then, I'm pulling a chair out, getting myself set.

There's a package on the table. It's gift-wrapped. Tied with a bow even.

Jill's pushing the package towards me. "I just had to make sure you'd have something to take with you. It's from Scott too, of course, even if he doesn't know about it yet. I was awake. I got up. I had everything I needed. You can open it now if you want to."

Why would I wait? Gifts haven't come my way all that often. Specially parting ones. Why am I fumbling at it? Being so careful with the Scotch tape.

"Don't worry, just tear it. To hell with reuse and recycle right now."

Tearing is in my skill set. Even from the back I can tell it's a picture. In a frame so it can be hung up.

No, no, it's not. It's a photo. There we are, all of us. *The Drowned Rats*.

I'm grinning my head off.

Jill's looking pleased. "It was such a good time. Want some cocoa?"

Cocoa would be great. There's something I've got to do though. I've got to go over, get the dishcloth. Wipe the F.O.'s off the fridge.

Almost worn away anyway. Almost's not enough. The F.O.'s have to be out of there. They have to be gone.

"Thanks, kid. I'm glad you did that."

No problem-o.

I'm sitting down again. Photo looks awesome. I'm holding it. I have it in my hands. Jill's got her back to me. She's heating milk in the microwave.

I'm opening my mouth because for sure, for sure there's something I WANT TO BE SAYING. Saying so she'll hear it.

Here we go then. Here it comes: "Even if I didn't have the picture, I wouldn't forget you. Either of you. I wouldn't forget my time here. I couldn't. There's been no place like it. It's been the best I've ever had."

Jill's turning sort of fast, the way she always moves. She's putting the mug of cocoa down so it's in front of me. Only she's slopping it. "Did I hear a-right?" she's asking me.

I am answering. "I sure as hell hope so. I want you to know I won't forget you. I'll say it again if you like."

"It's OK, I heard it very clearly the first time. I heard it and it means a lot to me. I know it will to Scott as well."

All of a sudden, she's got her hand across my shoulders. I'm not flinching. Seems to me massaging's kind of something else I could like.

Thirty

THAT'S IT, ISN'T IT? I'VE GOT TO TELL JILL. ABOUT THE CAR.

Hardly even thought about it for ages. Truly don't think she and Scott will care. Doesn't matter. I want to go out of here clean. I don't want them finding bad stuff after I'm gone. Sure as hell don't want them wondering if it was me or not. Rather they knew. Not much point in putting it off either, is there?

Gotta do it. "I wrecked something."

Jill has her hand on my back still but it's not moving any longer. She's holding it quiet.

"It was right at the beginning when I first heard about my dad. Day I took off. I found this old car. It's out in the fields. I threw stones at it. I'd have set it on fire if I'd had any matches. It's part of why I went to live in the loft. I thought I was dangerous. Only part though. I did want to be there."

"Scott and I know that."

"I thought I should tell you."

"That's a brave act. The fact is that car was here when we moved in. Who knows who it belongs to? Scott used to say we should try to sell it—not because we need the money but because it's a classic, an antique."

"Not any more it isn't."

"So I gather. I have to admit we haven't looked at it for quite some while—since you got here, I guess. We've been so busy. Walking in the fields seems to have slipped off our list of to-dos. If people value their cars they shouldn't go dumping them in meadows. It's where everyone round here seems to think is where old cars should end up though."

"I'd never done anything like that before. Not ever. I'd never even yelled at anyone."

"You frightened yourself."

"It was awful. Acting right's important to me."

"Don't think we haven't noticed."

"When I stopped…when I saw… It was like my father had got inside me. Like he'd taken over. It wasn't the same as when I took the knife to my thumb. I decided about that. I decided about writing on the fridge."

Jill's moving. She's coming round to stand in front of me. She's looking straight at me.

"You, my friend, are a person of courage. You, Kyle McGinley, are a hero in my book."

I don't know what to do. How to answer.

"For heavens sake, you're blushing!"

I know I am. I can feel it.

"Don't go wasting your blushes on me. You need a girl, you know."

I'm shrugging. Joke of the century.

"Your chances will be a helluva sight better too if you're willing to speak to her." Jill's giving me a grin. "You know what I think?"

How should I know?

"I truly do think it's time for bed."

Can't argue with that. I'm getting up, going to the door even. Better than talking about girls. Girls are such a sore point.

Only I've got something else to do. It's another thing too that won't wait.

So I'm coming back. I'm getting myself set so I can be sure I'll speak loud enough. Jill's at the counter again, her back to me. She's clearing up.

"I was wondering if you'd like to come and see what I've been doing. My painting. I was wondering if you want me to show it to you. We could go right now. We don't really have to wait till morning."

It's like she's frozen. Only for a minute though. She's looking at me again. She's smiling. Like I gave her a gift maybe?

"There's an offer I can't refuse, if ever I heard one. I'd crawl over broken glass, if I had to."

"You don't. There is no glass. It's only across the yard."

"Yeah, I know. But if I don't wake Scott to go with us, he'll kill me."

Hadn't thought of that. Be OK though, wouldn't it? "I'd like it but it's the middle of the night. He might not want to be woken."

"Are you kidding? You know Scott. He's always up for excitement and this is something we both wanted. We talked about it. How we weren't going to feel comfortable going up there without you. How we'd be like voyeurs. We tried to decide whether you'd want us to see or whether you wouldn't. We never did come up with a good answer. Now we don't have to bother. We'll be getting the gallery tour. You can say what you like, I'm going to wake him and I'm going to wake him NOW!"

Thirty-one

SO HERE WE GO.

I'm leading the way up the ladder from the barn bottom, lifting the floor flap ONE MORE TIME. Only I'm not coming alone. I'm coming with other people.

What am I thinking? This isn't any old "other people." This is Scott and Jill.

Jill was right. Of course, she was. Scott was about as eager as you can get. Came down like he'd been awake forever. Rubbing his hands together. "I hear we're going on an expedition. Don't expect we'll need the backpacks. I could bring them if you want me to—crampons even."

"Put a sock in it," Jill told him. Then we were out the door.

Last rung. I'm standing on the loft floor now. Scott and Jill are joining me. They've made it.

Lady C is not amused. She was settled for the night. Apparently, waking up again wasn't in her plans. She's considering us, giving us the eyeball. Guess she isn't going to be getting off her cage top, coming over.

"She's looks so healthy," Jill says.

"She must be, the trouble she's giving me," I answer.

Scott and Jill do care about her. Right now though they care about my paintings more.

Not that they're saying anything. Still, I can see it in how they're looking round. Way Jill's putting her hand out, stroking one of the trees.

I don't want them to have to ask.

I want to tell them.

"The trees are where I started. There's this swamp place. I went there in the moonlight the first night I slept up here. I'd never walked anywhere in the moonlight before. It's quite far. It took a while to get there. I just kept going and going until the track ran out. I sat on a rock then, looking and looking. I'd never seen anything like it."

"I didn't mean to paint anything. It had never crossed my mind. But when Lady C came—that's what I call her, you can guess what it stands for—when she came and she was so sick I was worried about her. I couldn't go to the window to look out at her one more time. I needed something else to do. And there was the paint. And there was this thing in my head I couldn't get rid of. Not that I wanted to. Anyway, that's how it all began."

"So the trees were the first?"

Jill's turned to the picture of Lady C now.

Scott's got his finger up to scratch where I've put her chin.

"Sort of. I put her up because I want to be remembering things. Good things. It's not just that though. I made her flying because that's how I want her to be. I want her to soar. She shouldn't be in some barn any longer than she has to. Her wing feathers are growing."

"You told us," Jill says.

"You'll have fun with her."

They're going over to where she is now. Moving gently.

"Will she let me touch her?" Scott asks.

"You can try. She likes that tickle thing."

Scott puts his hand out.

"Shameless hussy," Jill says.

Lady C's dancing for them. Hopping one foot to another. Lady C will be all right.

"You've done an awfully good job with her, you know," Jill tells me.

"I love her," I say. The words are surprise to me so I say them over to myself.

Scott and Jill have gone on to the storm now. I can see they're puzzled.

Time to plunge in.

"That one I did the day Scott took the photos of us. I was upset about something. Then the storm came and it was so big. The lightning filled the loft up. The thunder was like it owned my head. I didn't think even. I just had the brush in my hand. It's how I got to be Leopard Man."

"There's such a power to it." Jill's speaking in a whisper.

"Frightened me almost."

"Not a bad thing," Scott says. "Shows you know the need for respect."

"I'll think about that," I tell him. I know too that I will.

They look some more. They look at the storm a long time. They go back to the trees and the Lady C picture.

Takes a while for them to get to the wall by the window.

"It's a self-portrait," I say.

Jill laughs. "You really didn't have to tell me that, you know."

"I did the hair first."

"The hair is definitely a clue."

"But it's a good all-over likeness," Scott puts in.

"I only figured it out this evening. The wall was so bare. It was bugging me. It's why I came over early. Why I didn't sit around."

"You signed it," Jill says.

"Shouldn't I have?" I ask.

"Of course."

"But it's your barn."

"You've transformed it. What more could we want?" Jill seems like she's choked up. But also like she's certain.

Scott's squatting, peering at the picture of Ingen. "Who's the little guy?"

I've got my answer ready. "Just someone I made up."

"In other words, he's your business." Scott stands and stretches.

I nod as definitely as I can.

"No problems there," Scott tells me. "I must say I'm enjoying the fact speech seems to be on your agenda all of a sudden."

Doesn't seem hard. Not hard at all—to say it.

"I'm liking it too," I get out. "I'm liking it a lot."

Thirty-two

SHOULD'VE KNOWN MY DAD'D KEEP US WAITING.

Two thirty before Scott and Jill took themselves off. Back down the ladder. Couldn't seem to get enough of being with me in the loft.

We were still up early, all of us. Lady C had hardly started stirring. My eyes were wide open. I was twitching in every limb.

I thought I'd come slinking over. Being quiet. Getting myself some cereal. Turned out quiet wasn't needed. Scott and Jill were at the coffee already.

"Might as well cook breakfast," Jill said.

She made scrambled eggs again. Weird how it went down better. Seemed impossible, but it did.

When breakfast was over, I went for a shower. Washed my hair and everything. Put my Harley shirt on. Thought it might be lucky. Scott and Jill like it, whatever my dad may think.

"Helium would be better, of course," Scott said, but he was only kidding.

He never did show me where I could find that on the Net. I guess I could ask him to do it now. But I don't really want to. I don't want to do anything. Except stay sitting here.

Jill's baking muffins. I like the smell. She had to throw the first batch out.

"Forgot to put the sugar in," she told us.

She wouldn't even let me try one.

If I didn't have anyone to stop me I'd be at the end of the drive-way. By the mailbox. I did go down there once. Only I came back again. Jill made me. She called out to me. Maybe if she hadn't I'd have come anyway. It was pretty lonely. And I knew it was ridiculous, jumping at every sound.

The *Drowned Rats* picture is in front of me on the table. I keep picking it up and putting it down.

Jill's opening the oven. "Here's hoping." She's taking the new batch out.

Scott's going over. He keeps claiming he's going to go and check his email, but he doesn't. He's as bad as me. He isn't doing much of anything. Except now he's being the official muffin tester. "Nothing wrong with this lot."

"Thank heavens."

Jill's putting the muffins on a rack to cool. I'm getting one as tester-back up.

"Tastes good to me," I say.

"Right," says Jill. "I'm going to tidy these cupboards. You guys can keep still. I can't."

Scott and I are looking at one another. We're shaking our heads. We can't believe it. Jill's pulling all the pots out. Rearranging them. She's making this clatter.

"I could get you a few more climbing magazines," Scott tells me. "I've actually got some real classics. Hemp ropes, hobnail boots—the lot."

It's my signal to look up at the Himalayas. Hell, they're wonderful. The way the light falls on the snow is amazing.

"Climbing mags'd be great," I say.

Thirty-three

THERE'S A CAR IN THE LANEWAY.

It isn't someone for Scott and Jill. It doesn't have anything to do with wetlands and meetings. It isn't a delivery truck.

It's my father.

My dad

He's getting out. No problem recognizing him. Knowing who he is. Doesn't look much different. Same kind of sports jacket. Same pressed pants. Few more grey hairs maybe. More of a pot. Rest's identical.

I'd know him anywhere. Way he's looking round like he owns the place. Way he's swaggering towards the porch.

Scott and Jill have opened the door. They're ready for him.

He's giving them the once over. "Very pretty. I've always fancied somewhere in the country."

I'm standing back a bit. I'm waiting.

He gives a nod in my direction. "Kyle?"

I nod back.

"You've grown."

It's been eight shitting years, Dad. Did you expect I'd shrink?

There's hardly another look from him. It's like he only asked because he wanted to be certain. It's like he's checking me off against some list.

Whatever. He's in now. In our kitchen, pulling a chair out.

"A cup of coffee, Mr. McGinley?" Scott's asking.

"A coffee'd set me up nicely," my dad's answering, settling himself down.

"I'm onto it." Jill's bringing the coffee and the muffins.

We're all at the table now. Scott. Me. Jill. My dad.

Maeve comes. She plunks herself on my feet. I expect Scott to send her to her basket, but he doesn't.

My dad still isn't looking at me. He's into talking about his trip.

"There was a snowstorm in the Rockies. Can you believe it?

"God's own country, this is. You won't find better.

"Banff, now, it's a zoo but the setting!

"Never stayed in the Banff Springs Hotel before. Thought I'd give it a try."

He seems to have an awful lot to tell us. Scott and Jill are speechless. They can't believe how he's going on. About nothing. Neither can I.

I know it's all bullshit. Doesn't seem to matter. I can't help listening. I can't help being excited.

Could we just get on with this? Could we get out of here?

More he talks, more it's like Scott and Jill are disappearing. Like I can't hardly see them any longer. Like my dad's the only thing there is. I'm watching him reach out, take a muffin, cut it. Those big hands of his. Hands I've felt on my own body.

I still want him to notice me. I still want to take him to the loft. You'll love what I've done, Dad. You'll love it. That's what I'll say to him. I'm packed. I'm ready. I could go and sit in the car even. I could wait for you. Just tell me where we're going. What's your home like? Where is it?

I'm older now. I won't be any trouble to you.

My dad's mug is empty.

"More coffee?" Scott asks him.

Wish he wouldn't. Wish my father wasn't saying, "I don't mind if I do."

I've had it with delaying. I can't see what we're waiting for.

My dad's taking another muffin. He's still talking. His mouth's opening and closing. Words are coming out of it. Words that seem to have no ending. Words that are drowning me. Sweeping me along.

It's got to be time to leave. We've probably got a long way to travel. Why isn't he in more of a hurry?

Jill's getting up. She's standing with her hands on the chair back. "Mr. McGinley."

My dad's actually pausing. He's eyeing her. "Mr. McGinley." She's speaking very carefully. "I gather it's been a number of years since you've seen Kyle."

You can say that again.

My dad's annoyed. He doesn't like it. Being interrupted. "As my lawyer made clear, there were circumstances beyond my control."

He thinks that should be the end of it. He isn't expecting Scott to lean forward. "It's not our job to judge, Mr. McGinley, but we've enjoyed having Kyle with us. We'll miss him. We'd like to know something of your plans for him. I imagine he would too."

My father gives a snort. He leans back, lolling, one arm over the chair back. "I don't think it's any of your business."

"There is such a thing as simple human concern." Scott's not letting him off the hook.

"I don't have to tell you anything."

"Jill and I know that."

"Scott and I would just like to have some idea. We're aware we can't alter anything."

My father's eyes start narrowing. "I've met your sort before. You're two more in a long, long line of interfering busybodies. That's the polite word. I have others."

"Which we would be grateful if you don't use." He doesn't know Jill. He doesn't know she's coming to the end of it. "Busybodies we may be but we have been looking after your son. He's been with us all summer."

"Cry me a river. Doesn't matter what you've been doing with him. He's my son. I can claim him any time I want to."

So go ahead, go ahead and do it.

"If I tell you anything, it's because I happen to feel like it. What I'm telling you is this. I left home when I was sixteen—same age Kyle is. My father bought me a one-way ticket to the other side of the country. 'Don't you come back,' he said to me. I didn't and I did well for myself. One thing I won't stand for is having Kyle namby-pambied. I believe it'll be best for him to be out in the world. Lucky for me, right now, I had a bit of a windfall. I won some money on the lottery. Enough and to spare to do what had to be done. I could've come by plane but I don't have much love for bureaucrats. Coming the way I did kept everyone on their toes."

"I think you should know how hard it was on Kyle," Scott puts in.

My dad's still not looking at me.

Another snort. "If he finds that hard, he's in trouble. Anyway, he appears to be all right. Apart from the paint on him. Presumably he got that because you've been using him as unpaid labour. Not that I'm against it. Kid like him should earn his keep."

"Mr. McGinley, are you really saying—?" Jill's angrier than I've ever seen her.

My dad's not going to let her finish. "You can believe what you like. My next move is to get him out of here as quickly as I can manage it. The CAS has been after me for support payments ever since I've been in touch with them. How they've got the nerve I can't imagine."

"Mr. McGinley—"

My father's on his feet too now. "Get in the car, boy."

He's taking me with him. He is. He is.

"I have to get my stuff," I say.

"All right but hop to it," he answers.

He's smiling even. He's saying the words I've been waiting to hear.

I move Maeve off my feet. She doesn't want to go but I'm making her.

"You can say your goodbyes too. I'm giving you five minutes."

He's putting his hands in his pockets. He's jiggling his money.

Five minutes. Five minutes.

I look at Scott and Jill. All of a sudden I can see them again.

Five frigging minutes.

It's all of anything I'm ever going to get, isn't it? He's still not looking at me. Not really.

If he isn't paying me any attention now, he's never going to. Not when we get in the car. Not ever.

Worse, he's got that "little shithead" look on his face. Look that says he knows he can pick me up and put me in the closet any frigging time he likes. He can drop me off too, wherever he happens to fancy. Middle of nowhere.

I swallow. "I'm not going, dad," I say.

His hands are at his belt buckle.

"Get in the car. It's an order."

Everyone's standing. Maeve's at my side. Her hackles are up. She's growling.

"I'm not going."

"Who the hell do you think you are?" he yells.

I don't stop to think. I just let what I want to say come. "I'm your son. It's like you said. I'm your son and I'm not nothing. I'd be an idiot to go with you. You're the biggest jerk I've ever met. Thinking you can do this to me. This and all the other stuff."

"You get in that car, boy."

"If you'd looked at me, just once. Really looked at me. If you'd asked me just one thing about myself. If you had, it might be different but you didn't. I'm not getting in the car. I'm not even going to walk you to it. I've watched you do a helluva lot of things no one else could but I'm not letting you do this. Not to me. There's a way you're crazy. There's no explaining your actions. The tricks you play so you can have power over people. If I told someone else about it, they wouldn't believe me."

He begins to move around the table. Maeve growls louder, deep in her throat.

I think he's coming at me. I'm bracing myself. Scott and Jill have somehow got themselves closer to where I am.

Finally, he looks me in the eye.

"I was that little kid on the doorstep for a long time," I tell him. "I'm not that little kid any more."

"You can go screw yourself! You're not worth bothering with," he rages.

Then he's gone. He's through the door.

I don't move. I listen to his feet on the porch steps, the laneway. I hear him opening the car door, slamming it shut. He's revving the engine, squealing the tires, spraying stones all over.

The car's roaring towards the house now. We're all of us afraid he's going to ram it. I can feel the fear between us.

Right the last minute, he turns.

We go outside, the three of us. We stand on the porch steps. We see him heading down the laneway. A billion klicks an hour. He gets to the end. He doesn't stop. He just wheels round the corner. Luckily, there's nothing coming. We can hear him, disappearing into the distance. Then, we can't hear him any more.

We look at one another. Me, Scott, Jill.

Maeve jumps up. She puts her paws on my chest so I can reward her for her efforts.

"My own choice," I get out. "My own choice," I say.

Thirty-four

"DO YOU GET IT?" JILL ASKS. SHE AND SCOTT ARE SITTING NOW. They're on the porch chairs. I'm still standing, still staring down the laneway. "Do you understand what he was up to?"

"There isn't any understanding. He was just being my dad."

"Seems like you were right. Seemed like a power play, pure and simple," Scott says.

"Partly, I guess. He loves power, loves it. Especially over me. He'd have liked nothing better than to get me in the car, dump me off like he was always threatening to do when he took me driving in the nighttime, when I was little."

"He went to such lengths. All that lawyer business," Jill's shaking her head.

"It's just how he is. There isn't any explaining him. There just isn't."

"Do not expect rational actions from irrational people," Scott puts in.

That's a good one. A keeper. I give Scott a little nod.

I wonder if I should go over to the loft. Check Lady C out.

"I'm so glad for the way it's turned out," Jill adds. "We really do want you to have a home here although I am sorry too."

I stare down the laneway even harder. I know. My dad… It'll never stop hurting. I'll never not want it to be different. That's not "rational" either. But it is how it is. I turn. "Do you think we could have hamburgers, like when I first got here?"

Jill grins. "If you want the truth of it, I bought everything we needed in hopes."

"I am going to come back to sleep in the house soon. You do know that, don't you?" I tell them.

Scott frowns his joke-frown. "But we had plans to rent your room out."

"Too bad," I say. "It's already taken."

"Ah, we're training you well. No flies on you, boy-o," Scott rumbles.

"Could be too well," Jill humphs.

Scott goes quiet. "You were awfully good with your father. You made every word count."

"You hardly even shouted," Jill adds.

I think about shouting. "I might like to do it sometimes—shout, I mean." Pops into my head how what I actually want to do is shout right now. I don't say anything about it. I just start walking across the yard. I go to the gate. I climb up and sit on the top of it. I look out across the fields.

It's like it's all opening up. It's all in front of me. More than ever before. Ever, ever, EVER. The whole of it. The whole world.

I know I'm happy. I know, some day, I might be even happier.

I think about Ingen, Lord of Ingenuity. How he'd be pleased.

I feel the sun on me.

I think about Lady C. How she'll be up there in the sky one day. How I will see her where it's bright and blue.

I think about Scott and Jill. How they're going to take me climbing. I think how they want me.

I think about my paintings. How they're such a surprise .

I think about my father. The most miserable man on earth.

I jump down. I get my feet on the ground.

I do shout then. I shout loud. I lift my arms up. Over my head. I do these joy-things. The Olympic gold medal things. I give the biggest YEEEEEEEEEEE-HAAAAAAAH! YEEEEEEEEEEE-HAAAAAAAH! YEEEEEEEEEEE-HAAAAAAAH!

The biggest in all the world.

Acknowledgements

FIRST ROUND OF CHEERING GOES TO MY EDITOR, ANITA DAHER, who came up with the key change to the manuscript that allowed me to find means to give Kyle's journey its true voice.

Kudos then to my agent, Marie Campbell of TLA (Transatlantic Literary Agency). She had faith in the book from the start; she hung in and hung in—with strength and exuberance—through the difficulties of finding it a home.

Much of the final editing was done while I was facing a serious health issue. I would never have completed the task without the love and commitment of my partner, Jennifer Cayley, who willingly carried a huge burden and who became an even greater delight and mainstay in my life. My "offsprung," Mim and Kieran Andrews, and Kieran's partner, Dee Hutchison, gave love in abundance. Friends sent messages from across the country, boosting my spirits; they provided wondrously appropriate gifts and cooked so that our freezer was always full. Great Plains Publications made a crucial contribution, setting aside normal deadlines, giving me the flexibility I required.

Editing is, of course, the final phase. I am a slow, slow writer, needing space for more re-writes than anyone could possibly count. Residencies at Jane Franklin Hall at the University of Tasmania in Hobart and at the Centre for Creative Writing and Oral Culture at the University of Manitoba in Winnipeg eased the stress of this enormously.

A word must also go out to the three—now grown women—who came into my life much as Kyle comes into the lives of Scott and Jill. We have lost touch. Still, I want them to know they are not forgotten. It was a hard time for all of us but they taught me a great deal. I thought of them often as I was writing *Silent Summer*. I remembered the difficulties. I remembered too the bravery of their teenaged commitment to finding their own paths.

I have been a Canadian author of books for young people for over forty years. I know well how much I have depended on librarians, booksellers and educators at various levels to introduce my work to my readers. Final cheering goes to them.